TREASURE HUNTERS

Treasure in the Woods

E. A. HOUSE

EPIC Escape

An Imprint of EPIC Press
abdopublishing.com

Treasure in the Woods
Treasure Hunters: Book #3

Written by E. A. House

Copyright © 2018 by Abdo Consulting Group, Inc.

Published by EPIC Press™
PO Box 398166
Minneapolis, MN 55439

Printed in the United States of America.

Cover design by Laura Mitchell
Images for cover art obtained from iStock and Shutterstock
Edited by Ryan Hume

LIBRARY OF CONGRESS CATALOGING-IN-PUBLICATION DATA
Names: House, E.A., author.
Title: Treasure in the woods/ by E.A. House
Description: Minneapolis, MN : EPIC Press, 2018 | Series: Treasure hunters; #3
Summary: On the trail of a document that could lead them to a lost treasure ship, Chris,
    Carrie, and Maddison head into the woods in search of an old Spanish mission church.
    Except they encounter a stalker, a film crew that doesn't take kindly to unexpected hikers,
    and the vengeful ghost said to haunt the woods.
Identifiers: LCCN 2017949809 | ISBN 9781680768787 (lib. bdg.)
    | ISBN 9781680768923 (ebook)
Subjects: LCSH: Adventure stories—Fiction. | Code and cipher stories—Fiction.
    | Family secrets—Fiction. | Treasure troves—Fiction | Young adult fiction.
Classification: DDC [FIC]—dc23
LC record available at http://lccn.loc.gov/2017949809

For Victoria

CHAPTER ONE

"Accidents?" Professor Griffin asked, looking up from his salami sandwich in alarm.

Chris, feeling terribly guilty for disturbing the Professor over lunch, tried to explain. "When we didn't find anything at the church Carrie and I realized that there must be a parish register that didn't get moved to the new building, one that holds the key to the location of the *San Telmo*. And we're going to the site of the old parish to look for it tomorrow. Which is why I wanted to tell you about the treasure today. In case of"—he made vague yet (hopefully) significant hand gestures—"accidents." It was, as Chris had feared, really hard to explain his and Carrie's search for the *San Telmo* and have it make sense.

Also, Chris had hoped that bringing Professor Griffin an extra sandwich from the bakery that he really liked and surprising him with fresh muffins from the same place would make up for the fact that Chris and Carrie had cornered their oldest family friend in his office over his lunch hour and poured out a tale of secrecy, mystery, and terror, but the muffins didn't seem to be making that much of a difference.

"Yes," Carrie spoke up. "Accidents. Like what happened to Aunt Elsie . . . "

Neither Chris nor Carrie really wanted to get into detail about what they meant by accidents *or* what happened to Aunt Elsie, but they were starting to realize that just saying "accidents" to someone who hadn't had a near-miss with a car crash that wasn't really a car crash wasn't clear enough. Chris poked Carrie. Carrie swatted him back. Professor Griffin continued to look alarmed. "I think," he said, folding a discarded muffin wrapper carefully into a triangle, "that this is a lot to take in, smaller Kingsolvers. And you've been carrying this all by yourselves this whole time?"

"We weren't sure who to trust," Chris admitted. If Chris was being honest with himself, he still wasn't. Professor Griffin, at least, was trustworthy, though they might be putting him in terrible danger by getting him involved. But they had to, because who, other than Chris and Carrie, would Aunt Elsie have left her clues to? Chris was still a little—okay, actually a lot, but he didn't want to admit it—nervous about trusting Dr. McRae even as far as they'd had to already. It was only the fact that Chris and Carrie and Maddison were about to go into the woods looking for the ruins of an old Spanish mission church that had driven Chris to tell Professor Griffin why they might not come back alive.

The day before they had been, for once, hanging out in Maddison's house rather than Chris's. Mainly because Maddison had better access to maps than Chris and Carrie did, since her dad had an impressive collection of Florida topographical maps and was on a first-name basis with multiple park rangers. They had been debating whether or not to include Professor Griffin in their plans.

"Remember, he has a boat," Carrie had added, looking up from the map she and Maddison were poring over.

"Will you cut it out with the boat routine?" Chris had said.

They had been scattered around the McRaes' living room surrounded by maps of the Pine Lick State Park, and Chris had been sitting furiously on his curiosity for the past half hour because he'd never been in Maddison's house before. It was a small two-story, with yellow siding and a decorative glass ball in the front yard, and someone in the family liked decorating in green and yellow and hanging china plates on the indoor walls. Chris hoped it wasn't Dr. McRae, because the plates looked nice on the walls and he was trying *not* to find things they had in common.

"I'm sure we can find someone with a boat we can borrow," Maddison said. She was chewing absent-mindedly on the end of a highlighter. "Someone else . . . on this *island* . . . "

Chris shrugged. It did seem silly when you put it that way.

"Why is Professor Griffin the only person with a boat you can borrow, anyway?" Maddison asked.

"Because he's almost the only adult I can think of who's going to believe the whole story but not ground us for eternity when we tell him," Chris remembered explaining. Although now he was starting to worry about that claim, because the Professor looked—

"Don't worry," Professor Griffin said. "I'm not about to forbid you from searching for a lost treasure ship, that would be hypocritical of me after I did all that looking for the spy plane that sank off the coast in the fifties. And it would require me to believe that the tall tale you're telling me is true."

Carrie bristled at this. Chris opened his mouth to argue but the Professor, with a twinkle in his eye, stopped him.

"Just teasing, Chris," he said. "I've known you two

since you were wee tykes, by this point I *do* know what a lie sounds like in your mouth, and the infinitely more stammered sound of you telling the truth. Although you really do need to get better at organized public oration," he went on. "It's a valuable life skill that requires cultivation."

"I made *note cards*," Chris pointed out. But before his speech he'd shuffled them out of his hands and all over the floor, and *then* realized that he hadn't numbered them, and finally given up and told the whole story off the top of his head while Carrie sorted the cards. She'd interrupted a couple times to clarify, usually when she felt that Chris was not fully explaining things, but other than that she had let the story come from Chris. Though she had added a few note cards of her own, which couldn't possibly end well.

Chris had also glossed over Dr. McRae in his summary of their adventures. He still didn't entirely trust Dr. McRae, and Professor Griffin would pick up on that, and Professor Griffin was terrible at hiding his feelings at faculty meetings. Aunt Elsie and three or four of the graduate students that she often had over for dinner—to save them from Professor Griffin's belief that one could survive on pasta and ham for eternity—had emphasized that point, repeatedly. A meeting between Dr. McRae and a suspicious Professor Griffin would end, Chris was afraid, in Dr. McRae and Professor Griffin getting into some sort of fight, the exact nature of which he couldn't imagine. Professor Griffin was just absent minded enough to be secretly hiding a black belt in some obscure martial art he had learned in his study of ocean-floor geology—really, it could happen! And Dr. McRae was still far too much of an unknown. He could have any number of secret agendas, unexpected skills, or unsavory underworld contacts, and even his own daughter didn't know what his deep dark secret was.

That Dr. McRae was honest enough to *admit* to Maddison that he had a secret, dark past was, Chris felt, only a small point in his favor. He was not about to be swayed in his opinion of Dr. McRae just because he was trying to help his family. He *definitely* hadn't decided that Dr. McRae's contributions to the whole adventure were to be kept as secretive as possible in case someone was after the new archivist.

Totally, absolutely, definitely hadn't.

"But I'm not so sure I like the idea of you two going hiking without an adult," Professor Griffin said with a frown, and oh great, here came the stumbling block. Chris wriggled in his seat and put on his very best pleading face, which Carrie said made him look like a constipated kitten.

"It's just a weekend," he said in his best reasonable voice. "And we could probably do the whole hike in one day but Carrie got a new sleeping bag for Christmas and she wants to try it out."

"It's just the old Pine Bow trail," Carrie added helpfully. "Then, when we get to the far end of the loop, we're following the horse path all the way to the coast."

"Well," Professor Griffin said, "I guess . . . "

"And there's even a campground right in the middle, it'll be perfectly safe," Chris said. "The park ranger we talked to said nobody's even gotten shot in that state park in sixty years!" he added when Professor Griffin didn't look convinced, and then Carrie smacked him at about the same point Chris realized how bad an idea it was to mention park shootings. But it was true; after an afternoon of poring over maps and not coming up with a plan, Maddison had suggested they try calling a family friend who was also a park ranger.

"Oh, the old mission church," Helen Kinney had said, finally connected to them after twenty minutes of playing phone tag. "It's visible from the equestrian trail off Pine Bow. Someone wrote an article for the local paper a couple of years ago that said it was somewhere in the middle of the park, though, and even though it's not at all true that version of the story just will not die. We've tried to set the record straight but we *still* have people getting lost when they wander off the trails with video cameras." Then she'd gone on to reassure Maddison that Pine Lick was remarkably free of smugglers, drug dealers, and other reasons that teenagers shouldn't go hiking unsupervised, and that there weren't even very many alligators.

"But, Kingsolvers, you're telling me this in case you don't come back," Professor Griffin said flatly, and to emphasize his point he took off his hat, plopped it on the bust of Melville, and ran both hands through his hair. The result was surprisingly similar to the time he'd accidentally touched a live wire trying to repair *Moby*.

"This is more of a . . . of a precautionary measure?" Chris said. "In case we don't come back? So if we don't, you know to start looking really hard into the things Aunt Elsie did right before she died?"

Professor Griffin sighed. "At least let me come with you. I've got . . . only a week's worth of exams to grade, let me get that out of the way and arrange for someone to keep the grad students on track and then I'll come along."

Which was the other problem Chris had anticipated but not yet quite figured out how to prevent.

"I think," Carrie said cautiously, "that Aunt Elsie

would be very annoyed if our backup plan went and spoiled the whole 'backup' part of the plan by coming with us, and she probably didn't tell you any of this in the first place because it would put you in too much danger."

Professor Griffin stared at them for a moment, something strangely frustrated and nostalgic in his expression, and then he sighed, long and gustily.

"Well, blast and botheration, I can't argue with that," he said, and that seemed to be the end of it.

✗ ✗ ✗

"Why *do* you think Aunt Elsie told us instead of Professor Griffin?" Carrie asked later than night, causing Chris to yelp and almost cut his forehead on one of his mattress springs, because he was under his bed looking for his left hiking boot and she'd come through the window again.

"Carrie!"

"Sorry," Carrie said, and meant it, partly. "But really, Chris—why us and not him?"

"Uhhhh." Chris gave up on the search for his boot and maneuvered himself out from under the bed, to discover Carrie holding both his boots and looking faintly amused. "I figured it was because Professor Griffin *is* the logical choice for Aunt Elsie to have left a secret to. They were best-friends-slash-colleagues for years."

"Yeah, but then what makes Professor Griffin not a logical choice—"

"Well," Chris started, but Carrie cut him off.

"That doesn't make leaving the secret to us an act of—of child endangerment or something?" she said.

"You're worried about that body we found at the church," Chris said.

"Yeaaah, a little," Carrie said. "I'd feel a lot better if we knew who he was and if he was connected to this treasure in some way. But I'm *more* worried about Dodson dying the way he did."

"So am I," Chris admitted. "And so is Dr. McRae,

and Maddison, and Detective Hermann, and somebody called Lyndon who tried to call Dr. McRae three times while they were moving the body, did you notice that?"

"No, because I don't watch Maddison's dad as suspiciously as you do."

"Er," Chris said guiltily, deciding that Carrie didn't need to know about how he'd gone through the phonebook for Lyndons afterwards, and come up empty. Carrie tugged at the knot in one of the boot's laces, and frowned.

"What has me worried," she said finally, "is if Professor Griffin is the logical choice to leave this secret to, and Aunt Elsie gave it to us instead, and she did that *because* she knew Professor Griffin was the logical choice so giving him this secret would put him in too much danger, then doesn't that suggest that the person who killed her is, well, local?"

"You mean you think it might be somebody she knew," Chris said.

"Yes?"

"Which would mean it's most likely someone *we* know?"

"Yes," Carrie said miserably.

"But then who?"

"I don't know!" Carrie said. "It's kind of hard to look at your aunt's co-workers and figure out which one might have tried to kill you!"

"Okay, that's true," Chris agreed. "But—"

"Do not tell me you still think it's Dr. McRae," Carrie said sternly. "For one thing, we know he didn't live here at the time of the accident."

"I was *actually* going to say that it might be really informative to see if Dr. McRae and Professor Griffin know anything about each other," Chris said, since Carrie had forbidden him from saying what he'd been about to suggest. "Whatever reasons Dr. McRae has, he seems to know more about this whole mess than he's willing to tell us, but maybe he'd tell Professor Griffin."

"Or maybe they'll just end up arguing over the importance of the whale in *Moby-Dick* for six hours,"

Carrie pointed out glumly, and Chris had to agree that that was unusually likely when you left Professor Griffin alone with someone for more than two minutes.

The next morning dawned bright and breezy, with fate smiling on them for once in the form of a clear and unseasonably cool day. A light breeze was even ruffling the bushes and the palm trees at the trailhead for the Pine Bow hiking path when Chris and Carrie met Maddison and her groggy-looking father at nine o'clock sharp, backpacks, hiking boots, carefully high-lighted map, and excuses at the ready.

The excuses were a blind in case they were being stalked, and they weren't excuses as much as they were a careful evasion of any facts any parents might find alarming. Both sets of Kingsolver parents were under the impression that this was a totally normal hiking trip; Carrie had used the excuse of wanting to test out her new sleeping bag, and Chris had actually forgotten to mention to his parents that they were hiking with Maddison. Since his mom was the one who dropped Chris and Carrie off at the trailhead, this earned him a significant look and a promise of *talking* when they got back.

And neither Chris nor Carrie had told their parents that they were going to be taking the horse trail up to some supposed ruins, or that they were planning a little unauthorized archeology while they were there. Chris was still glum that they had had to tell Dr. McRae, but the man had basically known anyway, and as Maddison had pointed out, it was a very bad idea to go hiking and not leave an accurate itinerary with at least one person. "That leads to state-wide manhunts when you take a wrong turn and get lost in the cypress swamp," Maddison had said. "I've been told accidentally becoming the subject of a statewide manhunt is very embarrassing."

Chris had pointed out that their route was through a thick Florida pine forest with scattered islands of deciduous trees. The only swamp was a small cypress one on the eastern edge of the park that shifted to high grasses and palm trees at the coast. Maddison had accused Chris of being overly literal, and then Carrie had flipped a page in Maddison's carefully curated pile of notes and scared herself with a full-color portrait of the swamp ape, and they'd had to take a break to argue about the likelihood of seeing Bigfoot's smellier cousin in the woods. Swamp apes were basically Bigfoot, but with the notorious habit of smelling hideous, like rotting meat and barf. They were more common in the Everglades, and had never actually been reported in Pine Lick, although the next island over had experienced a rash of sightings in the late eighties.

"Besides, the woods are supposed to be haunted, not inhabited," Maddison had said.

Carrie frowned and sifted through her massive pile of opened-and-sticky-noted books.

"Wouldn't it then be inhabited by ghosts?" Chris asked.

"I was thinking ghosts wouldn't count as

inhabitants since they probably won't leave tracks or, you know, poop."

"Annie Six-Fingers!" Carrie exclaimed triumphantly, effectively ending a conversation that had started getting silly. "She . . . ugh, she grabs you around the throat with her unnaturally strong hands and squeezes until your head pops off. In revenge against the townspeople who chopped off her hands because they thought her extra finger was a sign of the devil."

"She squeezes people's heads off?" Maddison asked. Chris made the terrible mistake of trying to picture how that might work.

"If she catches you out in her woods at night and you don't heed her warnings," Carrie said. "First she moans 'my hands, my hands' at you, then she makes bloody handprints appear on the trees and rocks around you, and then she comes up behind you and grabs you with her cold, strong fingers . . . it's been a local legend since the 1920s."

"Is there any *truth* behind it?" Maddison asked.

"No," Carrie said, picking up one of her open books, giving it a quick scan, and then dropping it. "No." She did the same thing to another book. "No, no . . . Maybe, if we count a newspaper article about a six-*toed* murderer . . . And yes." She tossed the last book onto the pile. "But the one book that supports the legend cites the dissertation Father Michaels told us was faker than fake as a reference. And there are a whole bunch of versions of the story online but none of them are very reliable, and one of them looks like it might be about a ghost story from Ohio."

"But let me guess," Chris said. "Annie Six-Fingers is supposed to haunt the area we want to go hiking through."

"According to two of these books, the legend claims that her home was on the edge of the island," Carrie said. "And you can glimpse it from the Pine Lick equestrian trail."

"Okay, well, Annie hopefully *shouldn't* be much of a problem," Chris said.

CHAPTER TWO

CHRIS WOULD LATER INSIST THAT ANNIE SIX-FINGERS was the last thing on his mind when they started out that morning. Alligators were, although they were not likely to get far enough into the cypress or swampy parts of the park to come across alligators. But Chris thought that considering the strange things that had been happening recently, if they found alligators hanging happily in poisonwood trees he wouldn't be at all surprised. The heaviness of the backpack containing his sleeping bag, water, food, and bug spray was on his mind, because he hadn't been camping in a little over a year and he'd forgotten how heavy everything was.

And the fact that Maddison and Carrie turned out to *both* be the sort of hikers who went marching directly ahead with a purpose and set a pace that didn't leave Chris much of a chance to admire the wildlife was very quickly on his mind, since he ended up taking the rear more or less by accident. Carrie had gone on family hiking trips often enough to know Chris's ability to get distracted, though, and Maddison turned out to be the type of person who followed the recommended rules for hiking to the letter, so they never actually let themselves get out of visual range of one another. That way led to losing the slowest member of your party to be eaten by bears, and Maddison and Carrie liked Chris too much.

Chris and Carrie both had a very good instinct for keeping track of each other. Carrie insisted it was because she could sense Chris's terrible ideas, but Chris figured it was more about being able to tell if another person was near him. He was able to pick out Carrie's footsteps among hundreds of others; Carrie could probably do the same thing with him.

So, when Chris stopped short to investigate a strange flash of color he caught in the corner of his eye both Carrie and Maddison turned around and backtracked. Carrie, from the sound of it, stopping abruptly in the middle of the path, and almost getting plowed over by Maddison.

"You okay?" Carrie asked when she got back to him. Maddison was a few steps behind her, wrestling a water bottle out of a backpack pocket where she'd zipped it in too tightly. "Or did you find a painted bunting?" Painted buntings were somewhat rare Florida birds. Chris had done a science report on them once and yet hadn't actually seen one in the wild, so he kept an eye out for them whenever they were outside in the woods. But that wasn't actually why he'd stopped.

"Tell me you don't see a handprint on that tree," Chris said, pointing.

"Huh," Carrie said, squinting. The tree in question was several steps off the path and in a shady patch, but when the wind shifted a few branches you could clearly see a reddish, handprint-shaped smear on the trunk. It was at about the right height for an average person to rest their hand on the trunk. "Well it's a bit blurry . . . " Carrie offered.

"Smeared," Chris corrected.

"*Blurry*," Carrie said. "It's blurry, Chris, and it is *not* a bloody hand print from Annie Six-Fingers."

"Oh good," Chris said. "You said it so I didn't have to." He was very slightly more unnerved than he wanted to be.

"I think it looks more like a blaze," Maddison offered. She'd come up behind them and was squinting, her sunglasses perched on her head. "You know, path marking?"

When Chris continued to stare at the tree and Carrie to stare at Chris, she edged between the tree and Chris's line of sight and poked him in the middle of the forehead.

"Would it help if I pointed out that we haven't heard any ghostly cries about hands?" Maddison asked.

"Yes, actually," Carrie said, cheerfully ignoring the fact that ghost stories were notoriously unreliable, especially where fine details like the order of scary ghostly activities were concerned. "See? It probably is just vandalism."

Which was just asking for trouble. Or to hear mysterious noises in the woods, which was what actually happened.

At first it was so minor a detail that it could easily be brushed off. The day had started off lovely and quickly turned cloudy, the air still and heavy with humidity, and they had the trail mostly to themselves, aside from a family of six who caught up to them, and engulfed the three teens in chattering kids. (One offered them a bag of trail mix, and another complimented Chris's hat before pressing on ahead.) And they were only going to the midpoint picnic area. So, at *first* the law of averages said that the distant shrieking Chris suddenly realized he'd been hearing was coming from small children and he didn't worry that much.

Except, of course, when the second time someone shrieked faintly in the distance it sounded like it had come from somewhere *behind* Chris.

"Did you hear something?" he asked Carrie, after speeding up to catch up to her.

"Err," Carrie said.

Somewhere off to their left this time, faint but unfairly unmistakable, someone shrieked in anguish.

"Well, yes," Carrie admitted. The hair on the back of Chris's neck was standing on end.

"But you know what rabbits sound like when something's got them . . . " Carrie added.

Chris was going to say something incredulous about the difference between skepticism and willful blindness to the obvious, but Maddison interrupted them by winging the bag of trail mix she had been elected to carry at the space between their heads. She had good aim, and had been just around the bend of the trail when Chris had stopped, hidden in a tall tuft of grass, so Chris jumped a mile and almost fell into a trailside stand of trees when she did.

"Sorry," he said, once he'd grabbed at Carrie and overbalanced them both and been unceremoniously dumped on the side of the trail by a flailing cousin.

"Just chill. Just a bit, okay?" Maddison said, exasperated. "Before I snap and run screaming back to civilization?"

Belatedly, Chris remembered Dr. McRae sounding genuinely astonished that Maddison was willing to go hiking, and realized that she might not even want to be out here. And that jumping at every little noise, even if there was a *reason* to be suspicious of every little noise, was not at all the right way to keep a nervous friend from freaking out.

"I really am sorry," he said, attempting to help Carrie dust trail dirt off her knees. "I forgot to ask if you even *like* hiking."

"I like hiking just fine," Maddison said woefully. "I just don't really like bugs and the woods always seem to be full of things staring at me."

As one, and almost entirely by instinct, they all glanced worriedly into the woods in the direction of the shrieking. The woods continued to be a thick tangle of grasses and pines, with rich green deciduous leaves popping up here and there. There were a couple of smallish butterflies fluttering around the path. Everything looked sleepy and peaceful, not as though there was a ghost hiding behind a tree waiting to jump out and yell, "Boo!"

✗ ✗ ✗

"I'm pretty sure she won't say 'boo!'" Maddison said over lunch. They'd made it to the little clearing with picnic tables and a "You Are Here" map without running into anything more alarming than a girl trying to hike while texting. It had been Carrie's friend Hailey from debate club, in fact, and they'd had to stop and catch up, and then Hailey and Carrie had tried to recruit Maddison to the debate club. Chris tried to be inconspicuous in the background while they were talking, and decided that he needed to get a better service provider for his phone because Hailey was able to text in the middle of the woods while he only got one bar.

"Right," said Chris. "She's just going to pop up out

of the trees and shriek at us about trespassing on her property, and then try to squeeze our heads off."

There had not even been a whisper of a ghost among the trees, or unearthly shrieking, and they'd stopped at the picnic area just as the family of six was leaving it. So Chris *might* have complained about the noise little kids could make for a specific reason, that reason being to turn the conversation in the general direction of the ghost of Annie Six-Fingers. He was really hoping he hadn't completely ruined Maddison's peanut butter and jelly sandwich but the weird noises in the woods were scaring him more than he let on.

"But doesn't that *kiiiinda* contradict the fact that she's supposed to moan about her hands?" Carrie pointed out.

"Which is why I wouldn't be surprised if it's not Annie at all, but somebody trying to scare us away," Maddison said to her sandwich.

"Oh drat," Carrie said. "You were supposed to let Chris be the voice of paranoia so we could all pretend that there isn't a very good reason to be worried we're"—she dropped her voice—"being followed."

"Voice of paranoia?" Chris protested. "Hey, it isn't—"

"—paranoia if they really are out to get you," Carrie and Maddison finished for him.

"We don't *know* that they—" Carrie stopped. "We don't know why they would be out to get *us*," she amended. "The best suspect kind of died."

"Carrie thinks it might be somebody who knew Aunt Elsie," Chris said, instead of making a big deal out of Carrie admitting that he might be right about something for once.

"Well, that would make sense," Maddison said. When both Chris and Carrie frowned at her she added, "Cliff Dodson—the guy who—*you know*. He worked for a company that provides food service for a lot of academic institutions all over Florida, and I caught Dad on the phone with his police detective friend the day before yesterday, complaining about how many places use the same catering service."

"Police detective friend?" Chris asked.

"The archive only has a sandwich shop," Carrie said, because she was nit-picky like that.

"Yeah," Maddison said, "but what about the branch college that they do a lot of work with? Or the people they hire when they have an event that needs catering?"

"Oh, that's a good point," Carrie admitted. "I have no idea."

"Your dad is best friends with a police detective?" Chris asked, because nobody seemed to have noticed this yet. Except probably Maddison, since she'd mentioned it.

"Oh, him!" Maddison said. "Yeah, it's weird, I don't actually know why they're friends. Detective Lyndon is twice Dad's age, so he's retired, and he lives somewhere in Nebraska with his wife and a bunch of grandkids and a lot of chickens. But he and Dad talk all the time. Dad's been on the phone with him a *lot* recently, though," Maddison added, like someone who knew exactly why that was suspicious.

"So, somebody who needed to murder Aunt Elsie

paid the caterer to do it," Carrie said slowly, while Chris was still trying to decide how to feel about Maddison's most recent revelation. Maddison suddenly remembered she had half a sandwich left and took a huge bite. "And it's likely that Dr. McRae suspects, at the very least, the point of contact." Carrie stopped abruptly and looked at Maddison. "Your dad isn't the type of person to stake out a cafeteria in a terrible wig and glasses, is he?"

"That was one time!" Chris interrupted. "And Greg was being a jerk to you, and we promised never to speak of it again! Mom and Dad swore an oath on their lucky cowboy boots!"

"Mrs. Hadler told Chris that undercover was *not* in his future," Carrie told Maddison, as she *hadn't* sworn an oath on the lucky cowboy boots. Maddison looked delighted, but in a pleasant way, not a nasty one, so the story of how Chris had disguised himself and skipped French class so he could spy on Carrie's lunch period because one of the boys in her geometry class had been saying mean things to her wasn't as embarrassing as it could have been. At the time, he foolishly hadn't thought of an endgame—other than to thoroughly scare the guy. It turned out that dressing up as what Carrie had later deemed a "psychotic Inspector Gadget knock-off" and throwing your cousin's geometry textbook at the boy who had been calling her names got you in a lot of trouble. Specifically, a threatened yearlong detention, which was mercifully avoided when Carrie and Greg formed a lasting friendship based entirely on "Can you *believe* Chris does stuff like this," and Greg's mother didn't let the principal get all the way through explaining the situation before bursting out laughing. Chris's parents were thoroughly shaken at getting called in to a meeting with the principal and had been the only people upset.

Greg was one of Chris's closest friends at the moment, even though he was physically so far away since his mom had decided that a trip to France was necessary this summer, but that didn't have any bearing on the matter at hand, Chris explained. They could all just forget Carrie mentioned him now. Chris didn't think Maddison believed him, but at least she was kind enough to pretend.

"My dad would be excellent at undercover," Maddison said, still grinning. "He would never go with a terrible wig, though. And, um, I may have made him promise not to do any extra investigating until I got back?"

"Are you worried?" Carrie asked.

"I think your aunt may have given the notes and everything she had on the treasure to you because she didn't know who to trust," Maddison said carefully. "And if she lived here for years but didn't know who to trust, then how is my dad supposed to figure that out?"

Carrie gave Chris a significant look while Maddison was distracted by the trail mix.

"Maybe we should have put Professor Griffin in touch with your dad," Chris said. "We told him the same thing, except not exactly because sometimes he does this thing where he remembers *part* of what you've told him but not if it was something he needs to do or something he must never do and we didn't want him to think he needed to go out looking for trouble."

"I still don't know if they'd get along very well," Maddison admitted. She was picking the raisins out of the trail mix and leaving everything else. "Dad doesn't trust other people very easily and whenever Professor Griffin comes up in conversation he makes a face like he doesn't want anyone to know what he thinks, and I don't think they've ever been in the same room together."

"Do not dare suggest that they are secretly the same person," Carrie told Chris sternly.

Chris attempted to stare heroically into the distance.

"But if Cliff Dodson was hired by someone at a campus where he worked, there are at least three different cities that would point to," Carrie said to Maddison. "So, haven't we just widened our pool of possible suspects?"

"Pretty much," Maddison said. "And that's not counting the other places that might hire caterers, or the fact that we have no idea *how many* people are involved. But I wouldn't be surprised if someone was following us. Remember how my dad was worried that there was someone at the church before us? Whoever is after the *San Telmo* besides us might have been there since we left." Maddison bit her lip. She looked, Chris noted, uncomfortable with how exposed they were in the picnic area. "They might be after us not so much because we have, or might have, a clue Aunt Elsie left behind, but because they want to let us do the legwork for them."

Ah. Well, that would explain why he felt uncomfortably exposed in the picnic area; pretty much the only positive part of sitting alone at a wooden picnic table in the middle of a clearing in the middle of the woods was that they could see if anyone tried to get too close, and if they were talking quietly it would be hard for anyone to hear them. Provided, of course, that you absolutely discounted ghosts as a possible explanation for the creeping feeling of not being alone in the woods, which had not left Chris since he'd first heard the shrieking. And Chris was not sure he could discount the ghost theory yet, considering what he'd noticed while trying to stare heroically into the distance.

"Chris?" Carrie said, since apparently, Chris not joining in the conversation about suspects was suspicious. "Is something the matter—oh, seriously?"

She'd followed his line of sight to where a fat, not–poison oak grew just off the curated part of the grass-and-dirt picnic area. Someone had put another handprint on the tree . . .

"Is it just me, or does that handprint look like it was made by someone who had an extra finger?" Chris asked. Carrie groaned and put her head in her hands. Maddison, however, abruptly stood up and stalked across the short, cleared area, aiming right for the tree.

"Uh, Maddison, what are you"—Chris scrambled to his feet, sending his potato chips flying—"doing? The park service doesn't like it when people go off the trail or the marked picnic areas," he added when he caught up to her, studying the woods with a calculating expression.

"We're planning to sneak into the ruins of an old mission church," Maddison said, still looking thoughtful. "Let me see that napkin?"

"What do you need my potato chip napkin for?"

"I'm going to find out," Maddison explained, stepping carefully among the grasses and scattered leaves and up to the tree itself, "if this really is blood."

If there really is an Annie Six-Fingers she is going to be very upset that someone messed up her nice, scary handprint of blood, Chris thought a little hysterically, as Maddison folded the napkin up a dozen times and drew the cleanest side directly across one of the edges of the bloody handprint. Then she hopscotched back over to Chris and Carrie, napkin in hand, grinning.

"Not Annie," she said, handing the napkin to Chris. "Or at least, not unless Annie likes leaving corn syrup and food coloring handprints on everything."

"Corn syrup?" Carrie asked. Chris sniffed the napkin gingerly and confirmed that it did smell sweet, and not at all like blood. "Like, corn syrup and red food coloring, the traditional fake blood for low-budget horror movies?"

"Apparently."

"So, someone really *is* trying to scare us away," Carrie said, and all the relief Chris had been feeling from discovering that Annie Six-Fingers was most likely a hoax evaporated. The thick tree cover looked menacing again, and edging back to the picnic table suddenly seemed like a good idea.

CHAPTER THREE

"We have two options," Carrie said when they were seated again, finishing off the last of their sandwiches and watching the tree line nervously. "Head back, which would be the smart and safe thing to do, so we'll just assume that Chris is opposed—"

"Hey!"

"Or, well, continue, with the *almost* certain knowledge that somebody doesn't want us out here."

"Or hope that Annie Six-Fingers is actually real," Chris suggested. "If Maddison brought her EMF meter, we could prove that Annie exists."

"I . . . did bring my EMF meter," Maddison agreed.

She was rummaging through her backpack and being discreet about it; Chris wasn't sure if that was a good thing or not. He had never actually seen a Maddison plan in action before but he had a sneaking suspicion that she was planning something.

"Uh-huh," Carrie sighed. "Did you also bring your video camera, so we can leave a record of our tragic and ghost-related demise behind when we disappear in the wilderness?"

"We are not going to disappear into the wilderness," Chris protested, "and I'm sorry I made you watch that movie with me. I didn't even know it was going to be fake-documentary style!"

Carrie growled at him. She *really* didn't like violent horror movies.

"*Actually*, I left my video camera at home," Maddison said. "I try to only ever bring one expensive thing on a camping trip in case I fall in a pond or something. But"—she pulled a trail map out of her bag—"I might have a suggestion?"

The map was fresh but old, as though it hadn't seen

much use but had been printed several years ago, and when Maddison folded it down Chris could see that it was out of date.

"So," Maddison said, chewing on her bottom lip, "Mrs. Kinney gave me this map along with a really stern lecture about how you should never, ever, *ever* go off the path in a state park, ever, because if you do they might not be able to find you if you get hurt, plus you could harm fragile ecosystems. But this one right here is an old trail they're talking about opening back up so it's been hiked recently, so if we really needed to take a detour . . . " She trailed off, tracing a trail on the map.

At some point between 1999 and 2017 the Pine Bow hiking trail had been diverted around a clump of trees and merged with a longer trail that headed deeper into the heart of the woodsy part of the island. That meant that there was an abandoned trail that branched off from the Pine Bow path. This path left the Pine Bow path about a mile before the picnic area, crisscrossed the equestrian trail a couple of times, and eventually approached the ruins of what, on the map, was labeled "old cottage, still unidentified age and provenance."

"The only other person who knows about this trail is my dad," Maddison said, tracing a finger along the line of the trail. "But he knows we *might* take this route, so if we wanted to, say, act like we were heading back to the trailhead and then switch onto this trail, it might buy us a little breathing room?"

"How on earth did you get this out of a park ranger?" Carrie asked. "And won't she lose her job or something if we make a wrong turn and have to be rescued?"

"Technically, this map was in my parent's map collection," Maddison said. "I actually found it folded into a bigger map of the Florida State Parks and thought I could use it on this trip, but then I noticed the differences so I called Mrs. Kinney and asked about it. She said she'd rather give me safe alternatives than see me get hurt, and that she doesn't want to know what we're doing. If anybody *asks,* though, I did not ask a park ranger about the safety of using an out-of-date trail map."

In the end, they decided to go with Maddison's plan, primarily because Maddison was the only one who had come up with an actual plan. Although Chris personally thought that they should have brought a video camera so that if everything went belly-up they could at least leave a confusing and only partly coherent film behind as a record. Carrie proved to be of the opinion that she'd rather die unmourned and unremembered than be memorialized in shaky camera footage. They would probably have ended up arguing about the appropriateness of so-called found-footage horror movies in general, except Maddison interrupted to point out that unless Annie Six-Fingers was especially creative with special effects they weren't actually dealing with a ghost, and then it abruptly wasn't a fun argument any more. Chris had never expected to wish a gruesome ghost story was real, but he had the weird feeling that their adventure would be much less scary if they were actually being stalked by a ghost.

"Well, at least we would know who it was in that case," Maddison pointed out as they cleared the picnic area of any and all of their trash, filled their water bottles at the water fountains, and repacked their backpacks, then had a loud and badly acted argument about going onward or turning back that Carrie "won." And then they did turn back, right up until they found the old trail.

They had walked right past the abandoned trail on their way to the picnic area and hardly noticed it, though it was still surprisingly visible. The dirt and gravel path was overgrown and it had no sturdy brown signpost like the active trails, but the "trail closed" sign hanging from the chain strung across the mouth of the path was a bright yellow.

It was also only at waist height and easily stepped over, and then they were breaking about six different safety rules at once. The trail branched off from the

Pine Bow trail in the midst of a tangle of tall pine trees. It was overgrown, too, with ferns creeping across the packed dirt path, and branches meeting overhead and trying to block out the light. You could miss the spot completely if you weren't careful. Which was more or less what Maddison was hoping for.

They were quiet for much of the rest of the day; this path was rougher than the one they'd been on and it was a bad idea to chat while sneaking, and on top of that they'd spent much more time at lunch discussing secret stalkers than Carrie had factored into her schedule. It was pushing five o'clock in the evening and they were more than halfway to the campsite before Maddison dropped back to where Chris was taking up the rear and scanning the trees for handprints and asked if he really wanted to be on a ghost-hunting show that badly.

"Oh!" Chris said. "No, I have a friend who likes

horror movies and I asked Carrie to go to the movies with us—wow, it was all the way back in April—and I forgot that she doesn't *like* horror movies."

From her position several steps ahead, Carrie groaned.

"You invited me to a movie about Nazis in space," Maddison pointed out. "I'm surprised she trusted you to pick it out at all."

"It was a good movie!" Chris protested. Maddison hopped over a log that had fallen across the path and gave him an unimpressed look when she landed.

"Was it the one about possessed turkeys?" she asked. "Because I don't care what my mom tries to tell people, there's creative and then there's weird. And the movie about possessed turkeys and an eighteenth-century Thanksgiving gone horribly wrong is weird, not creative."

"It wasn't the one about possessed turkeys," Chris said, trying to remember ever hearing about such a movie and coming up blank. It sounded . . . interesting? Where on Earth had Maddison's mom found such a movie, and could he borrow it? "It was about a bunch of teenagers who go into the supposedly haunted woods to try to film the local ghost."

"It was terrible." Carrie had been farther ahead but the undergrowth was thicker and the light wasn't as strong, so she was taking more time to poke suspiciously for snakes hiding on the path and they'd caught up to her. "Nobody ever stopped screaming and the camera was so shaky you never even saw a ghost."

"I think that was the point?"

"If you're going to make a movie about a ghost there should at least be a ghost at the end of the movie," Carrie said. Chris was still not sure if Carrie believed in ghosts but he should have expected her to be irritated by a ghost story that didn't at least mention the ghost. Carrie was contrary that way.

"I thought you didn't mind ghost hunting," Maddison said, ducking under a tree branch.

"Oh, I don't mind ghost hunting," Carrie said, edging carefully past some poison oak that was reaching across the trail to a cyprus. "I just don't like it when expensively produced movies don't bother to CGI in a decent ghost! Anyway, there's a difference between ghost-hunting television shows and ghost-hunting movies and ghost-hunting documentaries and I only like—*ow*."

"You okay?" Chris edged around the poisonous shrubs with more haste than care and hoped he didn't spend the rest of the trip itching. Maddison followed a little less carelessly. Carrie was leaning against a pine tree, standing on one leg.

"Yeah," Carrie said. "It's just my foot. I didn't twist it or anything," she added when Chris must have looked alarmed, "but I think I landed funny. It's kind of twinging."

"Twinging like you aren't going to be able to walk?" Chris asked.

"Twinging like I should rest it for a sec," Carrie said. "Really guys, I'm *fine*," she insisted, starting to turn red. Chris realized that she was getting embarrassed by the fuss and was inching toward hostile so before someone got into an argument he changed the subject. Which he did by fetching the trail map from where it had been folded in his back pocket and checking their location.

"We're only about twenty minutes out from the campground," he announced, and was rather proud of how desperate he *didn't* sound. Carrie sighed and got carefully to her feet.

"You guys go, I'll be right behind you," she said, testing her weight. "And for heaven's sake, don't"— something shrieked in the distance, just like it had been doing all morning. They must have been in a valley because the sound echoed and Chris couldn't pinpoint a location.

"Don't find any ghosts in the bushes?" Chris finished for his cousin.

"Don't let your imagination run away with you," Carrie said. "I was going to tell you not to let your imagination run away with you."

"Well, you'll notice that I haven't run away myself, yet," Maddison said. "So I think you're good on that front." But she plunged ahead anyway, and even though Chris was starting to think it might be a good idea to head back he gritted his teeth and followed her, Carrie bringing up the rear. So that in the event of attacking ghosts she could turn and run more easily.

"How likely *are* we to find a ghost in these woods?" Chris still asked Maddison in what he hoped was a low voice. "Because you said you brought your EMF meter . . ."

Arguably it was lucky that Carrie was still a few feet behind them, because it kept her from noticing what they were doing—which prevented her from giving Chris a long-suffering and disappointed look.

In answer, Maddison swung her bag around and fished the EMF meter out so she could show Chris that it wasn't picking anything up at all.

And then several things happened in rapid succession: someone or something shrieked again, this time directly in front of them. A bright light flared up, so Chris momentarily lost his depth perception and his footing. And a section of the trail turned out not to be as wide as previously supposed and made an unexpectedly sharp right turn, so a startled Chris knocked Maddison over the edge and then followed her down into what proved to be a short tumble down a steep hill.

CHAPTER FOUR

As it turned out, Maddison thought with a calmness she had not realized she possessed, there was a third explanation for the suspicious ghostly noises in the woods, and it was "the travel-adventure-investigation show whose main camera man you and Chris just literally landed on."

Or possibly another member of the crew. Production team. *Actually,* Maddison thought to herself as a shell-shocked woman in jeans and a "Robin Redd, Treasure Hunter!" T-shirt offered her a hand up, *I have no idea what the terminology is for this. Help.*

On a more positive, or at least a less actively

disastrous note, it seemed as if teenagers randomly falling from the sky was enough to bring your average film crew up short too. There were about ten people clustered and scattered around a more-or-less natural clearing that was also housing a miniature tent village and a lot of camera equipment. All of them were staring at Maddison and Chris in some combination of shock and alarm. Several of them were dressed completely wrong for hiking, as though they had half an idea—but the wrong half. Of the group, maybe two people were dressed sensibly.

And one person right in the middle was dressed so distinctly that there was no mistaking the neon feather in the hatband of his hat, his shark-tooth earring, or his flowing ponytail. Or his blinding grin, although it was a bit forced. And what sort of person responded to unexpected falling teenagers by grinning like they were about to have their picture taken?

In person, Robin Redd of *Robin Redd: Treasure Hunter* was surprisingly tall. Maddison had always suspected creative camera angling, but the man really was that imposing, although the effect was ruined by the look of complete and utter confusion that swiftly replaced his grin, and also by the fact that there was a balding man with glasses in the background, shrieking and throwing a sheaf of paper in the air.

"Oh," Chris said, popping up to join Maddison. He'd managed to avoid landing on someone in favor of landing on a defenseless bush, had scrambled to his feet on his own power, and was now staring at the paper-throwing man with dawning comprehension. "*That's* where the screaming was coming from."

"Oh, don't mind Harry," Robin Redd said, striding forward and offering his hand to Chris in a transparent bid to stop the frozen staring. "He's just a little stressed."

The woman who'd helped Maddison up gave a pained laugh at that.

"Really, Bethy," Redd said over his shoulder, teasing a name out of Chris and Maddison before Maddison really knew what was happening, all while pumping first Chris's and then Maddison's arms up and down with more vigor than tact, although he didn't try that squeeze-to-establish-dominance thing some guys did. "It's just a rough week. He'll find Wi-Fi somewhere and have a long argument with the network and be fine. And anyway," he added, turning another movie-star grin on Chris and Maddison, "we have more important things to deal with. Like asking these fine folks where they came from!"

"Yeah, talking with the network will cheer him up," the woman who was apparently Bethy grumbled under her breath. She had a mechanical pencil shoved through her bun and the frazzled expression of some-one who had to do all the worrying for everyone else. "Perry, are you all right?"

"Yeah!" the guy Maddison had flattened said. "Camera's fine!"

"Yes, and you?"

"Oh, I'm good. I think I sat on a thorn bush, but I'm good."

"Hikers!" the man who had been shrieking in the background said, though it was more of a shriek, and with a lot of arm waving to the sky. He stormed over in a swirl of tossed papers and stopped directly in front of Chris, scowling. "Hikers! What do you idiot kids think you're *doing*?"

"What—" Chris started.

Maddison, who was out of the line of fire because she'd been standing closer to Bethy than to Redd, decided it might be a good idea to edge behind her. That Bethy let her do so with a sympathetic expression didn't say good things about Chris's future.

"What sort of idiots ignore the 'Keep Out' signs?" Harry demanded, stabbing a finger in the direction of Chris's nose.

Uh-oh. *This* was going to be tricky to explain, and to a man who was already furious about something, and also, Maddison had just realized that she and Chris had lost Carrie somewhere.

"We had this park closed off!" Harry continued. "Nobody is supposed to be on these trails! Does anyone respect the filming process anymore?"

Wait. Maddison blinked. They had been on an

unmarked trail, true, but there hadn't been anything about the whole park being closed.

"There *wasn't* any 'Keep Out' sign," Chris said, which was true, and although there had been a trail-closed sign instead there was no need to mention it to this very angry person.

Harry was taking an enormous breath in preparation for what was going to be a magnificent amount of yelling when Bethy interrupted him by throwing herself between the furious producer and Chris, fat black binder in one hand.

"Harry," she said gently, "I know you probably didn't register it at the time but I did tell you about this already, we couldn't convince the park service that they needed to cut off park access for everyone in the state so that we could film. And since we kind of need the park service on our good side or they might cut off our access to any and all Florida state parks, we told them that that was totally fine, and then you signed off on it. Remember?" She opened the binder and offered him a stack of papers clipped together.

Glowering, Harry snatched the papers, but to his credit—Maddison *hated* bullying and despite her and Chris being much more in the wrong than this guy she did not like how he was behaving—he got about half a page in before deflating.

"Oh," he said, scowling at the paper. "I see. I—this is—I need to go try to make a call. Bethy, if you could, er, politely get rid of these guys? And make sure they sign waivers!" he added as he wandered off in the direction of the largest of the industrial white tents, scowling at one of the papers in particular and dialing his phone one-handed.

"I'm sorry about him," Bethy said, turning back to Maddison and Chris and clasping her hands in a nervous gesture. Redd was staring after Harry in puzzlement and not paying attention. "He's . . . frustrated, right now. He's mostly talk anyway, and he's never successfully sued anyone in his life." She ran a hand fruitlessly over her hair in an attempt to smooth it and held out a hand to Maddison. "I'm Beth—call me Bethy, everyone does. Bethy Bradlaw. This is Robin

Redd, who I'm sure you've already met, or at least heard of—"

Redd swept his safari hat off dramatically. "Always ready to meet a fan!"

"The man you, err, landed on was Perry, our chief camera operator," Bethy continued, before Chris or Maddison could protest that neither of them would rank *Robin Redd: Treasure Hunter* in their top ten shows. "The guy who just stormed off was the show's producer and my brother, Harry Bradlaw. We're in the midst of shooting an episode of *Treasure Hunter.* And we'll be very glad to, uh"—she glanced across the clearing toward Harry, who was gesturing wildly on the phone, and set her shoulders—"give you both a tour before you go on your way, if either of you want it. Although if you want to make it to the camping area before it gets dark," she said, glancing from her watch to the sky, "we need to make it a quick tour."

"We do?" Redd had been fixing the band on his hat but he looked up at that. Just in time, as it happened, for Carrie to inch around a tuft of grasses, limping slightly and panting.

"So, I had to find a way down that hill that didn't involve throwing myself over the edge and hoping," she said, either so irritated by the events of the day that she didn't realize she'd walked into the middle of a television shoot, or doing a credible job of acting like she didn't realize she had more of an audience than Maddison and Chris. "And it took longer than I thought, and I—um." Carrie suddenly had an excellent deer-in-the-headlights look.

Redd was staring at Carrie in alarm.

"What . . . " Carrie said, looking lost.

"Carrie!" Chris said brightly and only slightly hysterically, waving a hand in the general direction of Redd. "Did you know that *Robin Redd: Treasure Hunter* was filming in the park this week?"

"*Noo*," Carrie said. "No, I didn't know that, why should I know that, I don't have any idea what's going on right now . . . "

Chris grabbed her by one arm and gently tugged

her over to stand next to him and Maddison before she spontaneously combusted from confusion. Television stars, it turned out, were the one weird thing Carrie couldn't roll with.

We had to hit her limit some time, Maddison thought. Her own absolutely-can't-deal-with-this was clowns, and she had a feeling they weren't going to learn Chris's until they were in some strange and unforeseen situation.

"Bethy!" Redd said suddenly, tearing his gaze away from Carrie with obvious effort. "We could offer them the spare tent for the night?"

"What?" Maddison said.

"Oh, that'd be great!" Chris said, grinning at Redd, because he was, as Maddison had very quickly realized when he spent an evening chasing ghosts with her, the sort of person who liked to poke dragons. How he liked to poke dragons despite *also* being the sort of person who was convinced that dragons went out at night to eat maidens she didn't understand.

"*Whyyy?*" Bethy whispered mostly to herself,

turning around so she could beat her head against the nearest tree. But then she pulled herself together and said, "Redd, why don't you show Chris, Maddison, and"—she looked at Carrie—"I don't know who you are."

"Carrie," Carrie offered.

"And Carrie," Bethy added, "around the set? I'll go . . . talk it over with Harry."

✗ ✗ ✗

Maddison had never been particularly interested in the filmmaking process, annoying all the people who insisted that a girl who carried a video camera around abandoned buildings must have an urge to monologue into the camera. And Robin Redd had always been more of a joke for her than a halfway-decent television host, but she had to admit that he was a shockingly good tour guide. He gestured with his hat just as much off the air as he did on, turned out to know a smattering of interesting things about every part of the filming process, and was obviously friendly with everyone, from the producer to the woman in charge of catering.

"Well, you see," Redd said, "the smart actors know to make friends with the people in charge of the food. Hence, Flo!"

He made dramatic-presentation hands just as dramatically off-screen as on-screen, too. The dark-haired, motherly looking woman he'd introduced as Flo swatted him with a slotted spoon but she was smiling, and she didn't defend her pears when Redd snagged one.

"Flo is also our nurse," Redd added as he bowed them out of the catering tent. "So, you really have two reasons not to make her mad. You know who can *really* do some damage if they decide to kill people? Nurses. They know all the right places to stab."

He stabbed the air with a pear to demonstrate. It might have been more menacing if the pear hadn't had a bite taken out of it, but Chris still looked back at the cheerful blue catering tent with a shiver.

"And that," Redd said, coming to so dramatic a

halt that Carrie almost ran into him, "concludes this tour . . . of the set . . . of *Treasure Hunters*. Join me after dinner for a sneak peek at what we're filming this episode!"

"It's Annie Six-Fingers," Bethy said, coming up behind them. "With a special segment on the Russian spy plane that went down somewhere over Archer's Grove in the fifties."

"Bethy, you ruined my reveal," Redd sighed. "I was going to be the first to tell them."

"You're going to be murdered by Karen if you don't go let her touch up your makeup and shoot at least one take of the opening," Bethy said, and Redd yelped and dashed in the direction of what he'd told Maddison, Chris, and Carrie was both the makeup tent and where the makeup person slept. She was also an assistant camera operator. It quickly became obvious that *Robin Redd: Treasure Hunter* was sadly understaffed.

"I talked Harry around," Bethy said to Chris, Carrie, and Maddison. "Or, well, I reminded him that if he tried to sue anyone they would sue him back for noise disturbances—he's been yelling all day, it's scaring the wildlife—and he simmered down and agreed that it's only fair we offer you a bed for the night. Well, a tent. We can put up a tent for you."

"That would be amazing, thank you," Carrie said. Bethy managed a smile for them.

"Let me show you where you'll be," she said. "It's a very nice clearing that's just a bit screened from this." She indicated the whole base of filming operations with one wide sweep of her arm. "We wanted one place to shoot Redd amongst the trees," she said. "And then I'll see if Todd wants to talk to you, he's always delighted to tell someone about how cameras work."

Maddison had a sneaking feeling that she was never going to be able to watch *Robin Redd: Treasure Hunter* without a certain warm affection ever again.

But it was also surprisingly obvious that all was not well with the crew of *Robin Redd: Treasure Hunter*. The camera crew were very nice but very jumpy, the producer was—well, the producer was Harry, and he quite obviously had a bunch of issues, and Bethy, who turned out to officially be the script writer, had dark circles under her eyes and the beginnings of a nervous twitch. And there was something very worrying about how small the crew of *Robin Redd: Treasure Hunter* (Redd, Harry, Bethy, the camera crew, and Flo the caterer who doubled as a nurse) was. It suggested that the show was in dire straits—and that the crew knew it. This was not a film crew that needed a handful of unexpected teenagers making life more complicated, and both the crew and the teenagers knew it.

Redd seemed not to be picking up on any of the tension, but Maddison sure was, and so was Carrie, and even Chris looked uncomfortable. But they couldn't just get up and leave, either. The sky was almost dark already and there was still the possibility that someone was stalking them through the woods. It was a shocking bit of luck to run into a film crew, and an even bigger bit of luck to be offered a chance to spend the night surrounded by adults with cameras. It put another layer—one with access to cameras and publicity—of protection between them and whoever might be out there.

Still, they were intruders and it was uncomfortable. At least it was uncomfortable to Maddison. As soon as their tour ended Chris managed to make friends with the camera crew and devote himself to learning the intricacies of halfway-decent film cameras, and Carrie politely took herself and all their bags into the promised tent to get a little peace and quiet, so Maddison was stuck, once again and by nobody's design or intent, as the odd one out.

CHAPTER FIVE

MADDISON STOOD AROUND FEELING SORRY FOR herself and irritated and lost for a bit, but it wasn't anybody's fault she was still the newest member of their little trio and Maddison had always been good at making friends, so she charmed two sandwiches and three pears out of Flo and tracked Bethy down. The writer had parked herself at the very farthest end of the smallish clearing at the base of a largish tree and was muttering distractedly over a script, but she looked up and managed a smile when Maddison knocked on the tree trunk.

"Oh, hi—and thanks," she added when Maddison offered her a pear and a sandwich. "Did I miss dinner?"

"No, but I have no idea when dinner is and you seemed kind of stressed," Maddison said.

Bethy sighed. "I was so hoping that you were going to *miss* that. I am sorry, you three seem like wonderful young people. We must all seem like raging lunatics to you."

"Not . . . all of you?" Maddison offered, because she didn't want to bring up Harry's strange behavior in front of his sister. Bethy made a face like she deeply disagreed with Maddison's statement, and took a large bite of pear.

"Todd drops cameras," she said, ticking off crew-members with the hand not holding the pear, "Liam is convinced that he's going to make it big by getting photographic proof of Bigfoot, Perry doesn't seem to register pain, and Robin isn't really in touch with reality most of the time—he didn't even think to have you sign the nondisclosure agreements I handed to him, did he?"

"No," Maddison said. Redd hadn't even had papers in his hands at any point during the tour. "But I won't mind and I don't think Chris or Carrie will either."

Bethy set the pear down to scribble a note on the script in her lap. "And Harry . . . Harry is a special case," she said. "He's really not normally like this, but I—I don't think I'm wrong if I guess that you've seen the train wreck that is *Robin Redd: Treasure Hunter* nowadays?"

"It's never been a show I expected a lot out of," Maddison admitted. "That's not to say I don't enjoy watching it or anything!" she added quickly, but Bethy was laughing.

"See, it's funny," she said, leaning back against the tree and setting her papers aside, the better to untwist her hair. "We finally got bumped off the ratings chart entirely by *Gator Grabbers* last month, did you know that?"

"No." Maddison had vaguely heard of *Gator Grabbers* but she really had no interest in a show about, well, grabbing alligators. She sat down on the ground next to Bethy; it made listening to her less awkward.

"And, well, the main *appeal* of *Gator Grabbers* is that it's a show that you don't expect *anything* from," Bethy said, neatly twisting her hair back into a ponytail and then into a knot at the base of her skull. "The problem with us, believe it or not, is that Robin still has some semblance of self-respect."

"So, you can't compete with *Gator Grabbers*?"

"So we can't compete with *Gator Grabbers*," Bethy agreed. She stabbed one of her pencils through her bun and twirled the other through her fingers. "Or any of the ghost-hunting shows. Or that cooking-in-dangerous-places show that's been getting really great reviews," Bethy added. "Although *they* actually have some self-respect, but theirs comes along with things like a decent budget and someone who knows how to advertise and a crew that isn't slowly going off the rails. That makes it easier."

"You don't seem to be doing too badly," Maddison offered.

Bethy groaned. "Last month we were shooting in the Florida Keys and we had to fire our safety consultant when Robin almost died of urushiol exposure."

"They got the poisonwood tree mixed up with the gumbo limbo tree?"

Poisonwood trees were, as the name very nicely warned, trees that excreted a frightening amount of the same stuff (urushiol) that was in poison ivy, except in much more impressive quantities. It literally oozed from the trunks of the trees. Gumbo limbo trees were nice, safe, ordinary trees that people liked to grow, but unfortunately they looked very much like poisonwood trees, especially when they were small. Mixing them up was understandable, but disastrous. And the sort of thing you tended to rely on a safety consultant to help you avoid.

"Wow," Maddison said.

"Yeah," Bethy sighed. "And then Harry threatened to shoot the safety consultant for ruining a week of shooting, so now I'm in charge of making sure the facts are checked, which is not in my job description."

"Actually, what is your job description?" Maddison asked. "Because being 'the only sane person' can't be in your contract."

"Redd introduced me as a writer and the show is supposed to be a documentary," Bethy said. "So that's a good question. I do the research and come up with a general idea of what Robin needs to talk about, because he's quite smart but his heart hasn't been in this show since about the point we realized nobody took us seriously. And letting him go off on tangents would be a disaster." She paused. "Or, you know, it might be so weird we'd get more viewers, who knows anymore. But basically I plot out a couple side bits that relate to the treasure he's looking for or the area we're in, research interesting things for him to stand next to, that sort of thing. Right now, I'm trying to come up with a five-minute bit on the ghost who's supposed to haunt these woods."

"So," Maddison asked slowly, "you guys are behind the fake bloody handprint we saw at the picnic area today?" She almost didn't want to know. The principle of Occam's razor said that the simplest solution was the most probable, and the simplest solution was that a film crew had added the "bloody" handprints for "atmosphere."

"What?" Bethy said, and Maddison felt the relief evaporate. If the film crew hadn't placed the fake handprint, then there was somebody out here who was—

"Todd!" Bethy roared, leaping to her feet and causing a cluster of cameramen (and Chris) to jump and then scatter as she stalked toward them, scripts and dinner both forgotten. "Did you scatter props in a protected environment *again*?"

Oh. Well that was actually good news for a change. Maybe Maddison should fall down hills more often.

✕ ✕ ✕

"So, Maddison turns out to have been right about the handprints," Chris said later that evening, trying and failing to inch his way gracefully into his sleeping bag. The sun had set and the mosquitos had come out in full force, chasing everyone into tents and putting an end to the magnificent whispered argument that had been raging between Bethy and Harry from the beginning of dinner and through three excellent ghost stories from Redd. They were having a difference of opinion about the fake bloody handprints. Harry had been of the opinion that a little manufactured ghost scare might be good for the ratings; Bethy had called him a number of creatively unflattering names. Redd had said something about the difficulty of getting red food coloring out of clothes and tree bark that both Bethy and Harry had ignored. The camera crew had sat around looking glum and chastised.

It had been a very uncomfortable evening—a lot like being invited to a friend's house for dinner, only to have the friend's parents fight about private family matters all through the meal. For once in her life Maddison was grateful for mosquitos—and tents. The three teenagers were now having a conference in the safety of a tent with mosquito netting, and the first order of business had been the elephant, or rather the ghost, in the room: the heavily debated topic of Annie Six-Fingers. And if there was someone stalking them who was pretending to be Annie. And if they had any idea who the mysterious stalker was. The general consensus, Maddison was sad to see, was "we still don't know" and "no."

"But you still think someone might be following us?" Carrie asked from inside her own sleeping bag. They'd been put up in the smallest spare tent, which Maddison suspected from the number of patches it had was really the backup tent that let in rain so nobody wanted to use it. They were lucky enough that it was keeping the mosquitos out. Come to think of it, they were lucky it hadn't started raining; the air felt about right for it.

"Well, does this film crew give you the same type of willies we were getting from whoever was stalking us?" Chris asked.

"No," Maddison said. Chris and Carrie both jumped and Maddison grudgingly yanked her sleeping bag open and poked her head all the way out. She was very fond of the fact that her sleeping bag had a drawstring, because it meant she could pull it closed and become completely cocooned for privacy. The only drawback was that it tended to make people forget she was still there. "Sorry. But there was something creepy in the woods, and if it wasn't the ghost and it wasn't the film crew then it has to be somebody else."

"Somebody like who?" Carrie asked, but she sounded worried rather than skeptical.

"I really don't know," Maddison admitted.

"Do you have a theory?" Carrie asked her. Chris finally got all the way into his sleeping bag and then realized that he was standing mostly upright. "Chris, there's a zipper in the *side*," Carrie pointed out.

"Why didn't you tell me before I got all the way in *this* way?" Chris demanded. He looked like a giant caterpillar with a human face, and Maddison thought about telling him he looked like an extra from a horror movie about human-bug hybrids. But he was also a bright, artificial-purple color and that just wasn't scary enough. Plus, she didn't know how strongly Carrie hated bug-based horror films. It was better not to risk it.

"Uh," Chris said, and Maddison abruptly realized she'd been staring at him and his bright purple sleeping bag thoughtfully. "What? Do I have something . . . on my face?"

He was possibly blushing, although the tent was lit only by Maddison's headlamp and Carrie's flashlight so it was hard to tell. Maddison *was* blushing, but it was because of a tangled collection of feelings about Chris that probably didn't even involve having a crush and so she was going to ignore them until they went away or became less tangled. There were more important things to worry about, anyway.

"We still haven't decided if we're going to go all the way to the old mission," Maddison said, fiddling with the drawstring of her sleeping bag.

Carrie groaned.

"No, really," Maddison said. "We keep getting sidetracked and I know it isn't anyone's fault but if we don't make a plan and stick to it we're just going to go in circles."

"Very scary circles," Chris agreed. He sat down with absolutely no grace at all, now halfway stuck in his sleeping bag, and finally unzipped the bag enough that he could get out and then crawl back in like a normal human being. "Especially since direction has never been my strong suit and I'm kind of hopelessly turned around . . . "

"We were almost at the campground," Maddison said. "You couldn't see it because we were going to have to hit the equestrian trail first and then double back a little bit, but we were probably . . . fifteen minutes from the campground when we fell?"

"The trail you two fell off would still work," Carrie suggested. "It's not like it peters out or anything, you guys just took a corner too fast and fell into—I think we're in a creek bed, to be honest. Or we could double back and find the regular trail." She pulled a trail map out of the pocket on her sleeping bag. "*Or*, I think we aren't even that far from the equestrian trail so we could take that."

"And let the headless horseman run us down?" Chris suggested.

"Chris, there isn't even a headless ghost in these woods, let alone a headless *horseman*," Carrie growled.

"Annie might be headless," Maddison suggested, and got to see Carrie throw her arms up in frustration from inside a sleeping bag. It made the whole sleeping bag wriggle like a caterpillar and did nothing to take Maddison's mind off bug-based horror movies.

"Fine!" Carrie said, after she untangled the drawstring of her own sleeping bag from her mouth and rubbed the elbow she had bruised for a full minute. "There aren't any equestrian ghosts in this park!"

"That's fair," Chris allowed.

"Shut up, Chris."

"I just said—"

"Christopher Kennedy Kingsolver!" Carrie exploded.

"O-*kay*," Maddison said, before they both started

using middle names and she was forced to reveal that her own middle name was Olive. "I think maybe we all need a little sleep. Do you want to continue this argument in the morning?"

"No," Carrie sighed, deflating. "I want it to be done with so I can sleep without worrying. Equestrian trail, regular trail, or the one we were on?"

"Umm," Chris said.

"Just pick one," Carrie groaned.

"The one we were on," Chris said after a long pause during which they were all either weighing their options or falling into a light doze despite their best efforts not to fall asleep. "So we keep being as unpredictable as possible."

"For once I agree with you," Carrie said, even though in Maddison's experience, Chris and Carrie tended to agree a lot more than they disagreed, arriving at the exact same conclusion at about the same time but from different directions. It must be something only an outsider would pick up on. "I'll go with the trail we were on."

"That's fine by me," Maddison finished. "We didn't seem to be followed when we were on that trail, did you notice?"

"Hm," was the only response she got from Carrie, who had already fallen mostly asleep. Maddison looked across the sleeping-bag lump to Chris and raised an eyebrow.

"She doesn't like staying up past eleven thirty," Chris whispered, nodding at the digital clock he had hooked over the tent flap, which read twelve thirty in glowing green letters.

"Well then, good night," Maddison told him, and carefully snuggled far enough into her sleeping bag that the outside world went away.

CHAPTER SIX

MADDISON WOKE TO FAINT SUNLIGHT, GENTLE BIRD chirps, and hysterical screaming. "What the hey?" she said, fighting her way out of the sleeping bag and wondering if the stick she'd had under her hip all night would make a decent weapon. It had been a weapon against sleep for at least two hundred sheep, by Maddison's count, but painful lumps on the ground when you were sleeping outdoors sometimes turned out to be the size of peas when you moved your sleeping bag the next morning. She would have to move the sleeping bag to see.

In the meantime, Maddison opened her eyes and sat

up in the morning sunlight, wondering what the yelling was about. Carrie was still a sleeping-bag lump, and was to all appearances actually still asleep, but Chris was pressed up against the zippered tent flap, listening intently with a frown on his face, and sporting the most magnificent bedhead Maddison had ever seen in her life. *Uh oh,* Maddison thought, one hand going to her head automatically, *how bad is mine?*

"How bad is it?" she asked Chris in a whisper, finding the hairbrush in her bag and starting on her hair. A second later she realized she could have been asking about the yelling *or* about her hair, but Chris was a polite person who didn't tease you for having birds' nests on your head when you woke up.

"Mm," Chris said. "You don't sleepwalk, do you? Or cook whole meals or clean the house while you're asleep?"

"No . . . " Maddison said. She'd never sleepwalked; sometimes she talked in her sleep but only when very stressed or sick.

"Because I don't and Carrie doesn't. And um, we might be in trouble."

"Oh no, what now?"

"Well," Chris said, as the shouting got louder and closer. "Apparently sometime last night somebody drenched three of the cameras in soda and broke all but one of the tripods and did a bunch of damage to a handful of other things. Harry did a lot of screaming about them too," he said. "But I didn't follow everything the camera operators told me yesterday so I don't understand what they did to the rest of the stuff. And as the only unknown variables . . . "

"Oh *great,*" Maddison said, just as Harry started to rip their tent flap open and Bethy basically tackled him and finally—finally!—Carrie sighed and blinked awake.

"Wha' matter?" she mumbled, squinting. Chris gestured helplessly. Harry roared something about "destruction of property" and then yelped like Bethy had smacked him, and the booming voice of Robin

Redd suddenly joined in the fray, offering Harry a coffee.

"Everything will be better if you have a nice cup or two and commune with nature for a bit!" Maddison heard Redd say. Then there was a scuffling sound and Redd said, "My *coffee!*"

Maddison and Chris exchanged worried looks. Harry was, it seemed, not in the mood to let coffee and nature calm him.

"Maybe you should just go back to sleep," Maddison told Carrie.

But Carrie turned out to be one of those people who went from fast asleep to wide awake and horrifyingly competent in no time at all, so by the time Maddison had put her hair up in a tight braid and laced her hiking boots back on, Carrie was neat and put together and entirely awake, and actually able to smile at Bethy and open the tent flap to her when she knocked.

"Hey guys," Bethy said. She looked tired and sounded stressed and had a very new coffee stain on her jeans. "I hope I didn't wake you up, but we've got a bit of a situation we need to ask you about."

"Yeah, we heard," Chris said. "Carrie, *where is my other shoe?*"

"Right behind you!" Carrie said, French-braiding her hair with her eyes closed.

Maddison fished an only-slightly-frayed purple ribbon out of her bag and tied it to the end of her braid, because she needed a little extra something today. Then she took a deep breath, set her shoulders, and followed Chris out of the tent.

It was a very sorry group that was clustered around the one aluminum picnic table, heaped with busted camera equipment and cups of coffee in the early morning light, but they were thankfully not a group inclined to blame anyone. Harry very clearly wanted to jump right to the point where he accused everyone of stealing and sabotage and just as clearly had been sat on by Redd, but he was the exception, not the norm. Much of the camera crew looked as though this was nothing more than what they expected, and Bethy just looked like she had a never-ending headache. Even Flo seemed subdued, but that was because she had obviously been dragged out of a sound sleep by people commandeering her coffee pot. She was still wrapped in a flannel housecoat, looking disapproving and somehow not nearly as silly as she ought to. She was also standing guard over the coffee pot, which might have been why half the film crew looked so mournful.

"Right," Bethy said, once everyone was awkwardly sitting around the picnic table either clutching a cup of coffee or staring mournfully at the ruined camera equipment or doing both or, in a few cases, staring mournfully at an empty cup of coffee. "So. Obviously we have a situation, and obviously Harry is in no fit state to deal with this." She paused to tell Harry—who had opened his mouth to protest or just start yelling again—to hush. "I know you're the producer, but you were yelling gibberish this morning—so I'm afraid you're stuck with me." She sighed and dumped a long stream of sugar into her cup of coffee. "We really can't afford any more legal drama, after Harry tried to shoot and then sue Susan last month." She glanced at her watch. "It's five forty-five in the morning, what were you even doing up this early?"

Harry mumbled something that Maddison didn't catch and Bethy didn't seem to think worth catching.

"So we are going to accurately assess the damages, call the insurance company, and see what our policy says about this sort of thing, and get what we *can* set up for today's shoot, and then—then!—we will reconvene at seven and have something to eat before we address the elephant in the room. Okay?"

There was a lot of sheepish muttering and then everyone scattered, but Bethy grabbed Chris before he could book it and Maddison and Carrie hung behind for moral support. And because Bethy would clearly have grabbed one of them if they'd been within range.

"I really don't think you kids had anything to do with this," Bethy said, "but I'd still like you to hang around until seven. I still have to get you to sign waivers since you've technically been on set and Redd has no short-term memory," she said. "I'm hoping to have an idea of who did this before seven anyway."

"Okay, we can do that," Carrie agreed. Chris nodded frantically. Maddison shrugged, because she thought that waiting until seven was the least they could do.

When Bethy had gone off in the direction of her phone, Maddison turned to Chris and Carrie and opened her mouth to ask if the *timing* of this mess seemed a little suspicious but Chris beat her to it.

"You don't think this was *because* of us, do you?" he asked. "That whoever is following us decided to teach us a lesson about hiding from them?"

"Maybe?" Carrie said. "It seems like a strange way to go about it. Honestly, this seems like someone is trying to keep the ghost story alive."

"But we decided that wasn't real," Chris said. "And this film crew *also* decided that it wasn't real, remember the argument about fake bloody handprints last night?"

Maddison did in fact remember the argument, as it had been a huge relief when Todd finally admitted, in the face of a furious Bethy, that he had planted the bloody handprint at the picnic area to scare Liam and see how long it took Redd to realize that the print wasn't real.

"Yeah," Carrie said. "But if we hadn't known that, what would 'a film crew goes out into the woods to shoot a documentary about a ghost, but all their equipment gets smashed' sound like to you?"

"The start of a movie that you don't like very much," Maddison said. "Ohhh, I see. Though I really wish I didn't. Chris, what do you—Chris?"

Chris was staring into space again. He had his "I've just had a thought, and nobody is going to like it" face on.

"Smashed equipment," Chris said thoughtfully. "Except not *all* of it was smashed, was it?" They were still next to the picnic table that had been piled with ruined camera equipment—which had been spirited away by the camera operators in an effort to see what could be fixed. Chris turned to stare at the place where the camera equipment had been, expression thoughtful.

"No," Carrie said slowly, "not *all* of it was smashed, but then I guess the ghost got distracted or heard someone coming and had to book it before she was finished."

"Yeah, and that's another point," Chris agreed, now looking both thoughtful and excited. It was the face he had when he'd just caught a clue, and Maddison, who was starting to suspect where he was going with this, felt a swoop of dread mixed with excitement. And she wasn't at all surprised when the next words out of Chris's mouth were, "I need to go talk to the camera operators!"

"This is not going to end well," Carrie said as her cousin skipped across the clearing to the tent with the second-loudest swearing coming from it. The camera operators weren't watching their language but Harry and Bethy were even louder. They were hopefully talking to one another, because swearing that badly at an insurance claims investigator would surely guarantee a denial. "And are you thinking what I'm thinking?"

"I know nothing about cameras," Maddison offered.

"But does the fact that at least one was untouched and only specific pieces of the equipment were damaged suggest that this was an inside job?"

"I was actually thinking we should go gather up all our stuff and check it for any extras," Carrie said. "I wouldn't put it past the 'ghost' to try framing us. But as far as the sabotage goes I think you're probably right, and I hope Chris doesn't find us another conspiracy that won't go away."

"Well, how bad could it be in comparison to what we're already dealing with?" Maddison asked.

The answer, it turned out, was not very. It was a completely ordinary, run-of-the-mill sort of conspiracy, and nothing at all like a lost treasure ship and a murdered aunt. Honestly, it was almost cute. Maddison was so shocked that she dropped her backpack on Chris's foot so that his explanation of what he meant was delayed while he hopped around in pain for a while.

"What did you put in here? Rocks?" Chris gasped.

"No," Maddison said. "Just clothes. And maps. And some snacks, and a really nice stick I think I could do some damage with." It was the stick that had been digging into her hip for half the night, actually. Maddison had found it when she and Carrie had taken down the tent so the film crew didn't have to, which they'd done after checking all their things for any object that didn't belong to them before packing everything up.

They'd gotten the sleeping bags together and it had occurred to Carrie that polite guests left no sign that they were there and she'd insisted on taking the tent down. It had almost come down on top of Maddison's head—the thing was unwieldy once you started unpegging it. She was pretty sure Carrie had polite guest rules mixed up with polite *camping* rules. Also they were just a little bored and full of nervous energy. They'd even gone ahead and packed up all Chris's things since he'd still been asking the camera operators nosey questions.

"Did you grab *me* a stick?" Chris asked. When he had finally turned up, Carrie and Maddison had been sitting on the ground playing a clapping game in the spot where the tent *used* to stand and feeling a little too discreetly tucked away. The tiny clearing was in the shape of a figure eight, with one loop far smaller than the other, and in the smaller loop there was just enough room for one extra tent and a picnic table, covered in bits of old brick for reasons Redd had not known when he'd given them the tour.

It was separate without being out of hearing distance of the rest of the camp, and Maddison was pretty sure they'd been put up there because of a combination of politeness and them being much younger than most of the crew. Unfortunately, there was a pine tree half-blocking sightlines to the rest of the camp and it was going to be hard to prove that they'd been in their tent the whole time doing nothing but sleeping. And the cameras were just through the bushes at the other end of the bottleneck, so they were still close enough to fall under suspicion.

"No, but I'm sure you can find one of your own," Maddison said.

"After you tell us that you didn't traumatize the camera operators too badly," Carrie added.

Chris agreeably sat down across from her, on a tree stump marking the boundary between the woods and the clearing, and started poking through the available sticks. "The funny thing is," he said, "if we did destroy the cameras we'd have been doing them a favor. They've still got the newest one, and the night-vision one. Those were the cameras with insurance policy issues. Everything else is insured, so according to Todd if they get an insurance payout they might actually be able to buy *better* cameras. And they can still finish this shoot, even, although it's going to be a huge hassle because of the tripods."

"Fancy that," Carrie said lightly. "Insurance fraud."

"But by someone other than the camera operators," Chris said. "They're angry about this. Like, really angry. Whoever wrecked the equipment only had a vague sense of what was useful and what wasn't and they got a couple things wrong. It's like I tried to wreck the cameras based entirely on the one tour I got last night."

"Maybe don't tell anyone else that," Maddison said. "We're trying to be as unsuspicious as possible."

"Uh, right." Chris looked automatically to Carrie, who was normally the person who yelled at him for that sort of thing, but Carrie was a little busy staring worriedly off into space. "Carrie?" Chris asked.

"You said that they only hit the stuff that the insurance would cover?" Carrie said slowly. "Like, maybe, they *knew* the stuff the insurance would cover and the stuff it wouldn't?"

"Yeah."

"But they also didn't know that much about cameras?"

"Yeah," Chris agreed.

"Do any of the camera operators know what stuff the insurance will cover?" Carrie asked.

"They know in general," Chris said, "but Todd was really freaked out about the one handheld camera until Bethy told him it was covered in the new policy—they

101

just updated their insurance a couple months ago. I don't think anyone really knows except for Harry and maybe Redd, and Bethy's going over the forms right now so she will after today—oh," he said when something crashed in the bushes behind him. "So," Chris said, "that would mean . . . um . . . aside from us, guess who didn't share a tent with anyone?"

"Redd?"

Chris blinked and nodded. "Right," he agreed. "But I actually meant Harry? Who knows exactly what the insurance will cover and what it won't and what's covered under the changed policy, and who doesn't have the same scruples that Bethy does or the relaxed attitude that Redd does, and who would have a pretty good incentive for getting that insurance money. He'd probably put it right back into the show," Chris added, warming to his subject. "He really seems to care about the show in a twisted sort of way." He noticed Carrie looking at him in horror and a second later realized why. "He's right behind me, isn't he?" he asked.

"Yeah," Carrie said faintly. "And he's got a gun, so don't move, okay?"

CHAPTER SEVEN

I<small>T HAD HAPPENED TOO FAST TO WARN</small> C<small>HRIS, THAT</small> was the problem: one moment there had been nobody in the clearing but the three of them and the next Harry Bradlaw had fought his way out of one of the bushes, eyes wild and gun in hand.

The bushes, Maddison thought, *I knew they weren't supposed to be moving like that.* And then, because her recent life experiences were weighing on her more than she had realized, *Why did it have to be* guns *again?*

"Okay," she said out loud, because Chris shouldn't have to negotiate while that close to a crazed guy with a gun, and Carrie was maybe starting to hyperventilate a little bit. "Okay, Harry? Mister Bradlaw? I know you're upset. Do you want to . . . talk about it?"

Stay calm, stay calm, stay calm, she told herself. *And invest in hostage negotiation training if you survive this.*

But apparently the producer took that as an encouragement because he took a gasping breath and launched into a stream of hysterical babble while Maddison tried to figure out a good way to get help before the situation deteriorated. Deteriorated more than it already had, that was.

"This is my life! Do you understand that?" Harry said. He was looming over Chris, and Maddison couldn't decide if it was a good thing or a bad thing that he was shaking too hard to hold the gun steady. The good thing was that he was only pointing the gun at Chris half the time, but the bad thing was that if he decided to start shooting he could hit any one of them. He could even hit himself. "This is my *life,*" Harry continued, "and it's going down the toilet because of those stupid alligators!"

"Yes, the alligators are terrible," Maddison agreed

frantically. Harry actually met her gaze for a second, before swinging the gun around and firing a shot into the woods behind him. Carrie and Maddison both flinched. Chris, admirably, did not. "Alligators!" Harry screamed. "Nobody actually wants to see a person grab an alligator! But they *think* they do, oh yes, they *think* they do, because that idiot Penderson likes them and he gives them *all the funding*! And I can't get around them or prove them wrong because nobody on this flipping crew has ever heard of competition! I *had* to do *something* to get us back in the headlines and keep us from going bankrupt! I needed to do something or—"

Maddison had been staring at Harry, trying to see if he would make a move to back off or if she could get Chris away from him. But she still jumped a mile when a dark form came tearing out of the woods and tackled Harry to the ground.

Chris threw himself out of the way and toward Carrie and Maddison, and the gun Harry had been waving went flying in a low arc and Carrie scooped it up. It sounded like she ejected the magazine and cleared the bullet out of the chamber, but Maddison was too busy stumbling backward, shocked, to notice. And then they were standing in a scared huddle, staring at Robin Redd and the man he'd just effortlessly tackled.

That's the problem with the woods, Maddison thought distantly, rather than deal with the problem in front of her. *Wayyy too easy to hide in them.*

"He's out cold," the B-list television star in question said. Redd's aim had been perfect and his voice was steady but the hands that pushed his hair out of his eyes were shaking. "Must have tackled him a little too hard, but I needed to make sure he *stayed* down. Are you all right?"

He looked smaller, sitting on the ground practically on top of Harry with his hair falling over his face and his shirt half untucked. He also looked somehow more solid and more like someone you could rely on. And stricken, because it was obvious that Redd liked Harry and it was equally obvious that he liked him for much more than just the show. Or for show business.

"I was afraid something like this would happen," Redd said sadly while Maddison just stared at him and Chris and Carrie chose to clutch each other in shock instead of telling him that they were both all right. "He's been acting erratic and irritable since *Gator Grabbers* started getting popular and I knew the bolt cutters were a warning sign, but I just . . . " Redd sighed. "Nobody ever expects it to be your own producer," he explained sadly, just as Bethy came skidding to a stop next to Chris with the rest of the crew a half step behind her.

"We heard a gunshot!" one of the camera crew said breathlessly. "What hap—no!"

"*Harry!*" Bethy cried, dropping to her knees next to the prone form of her brother. She was white as a sheet.

"Hey, no, it's okay," Redd told her. "He's not dead. He's just unconscious."

"I'm—I'm not sure that's any better," Bethy said

faintly. Redd put an arm around her and she leaned into him, shaking, for a single second. Then she shook herself and looked up at Chris, Carrie, and Maddison. "And you—are you three all right? He didn't *hurt* you, did he?"

"Oh!" Maddison said. "Um."

"He was just . . . " Carrie tried. Truth be told, Maddison was stuck between panicking about the fact that Harry had just tried to *shoot* them and desperately assuring everyone that they were totally and completely fine, so that nobody called the police over what was looking more and more like a nervous breakdown. She got the feeling Carrie was stuck in the same dilemma, and turned to Chris. She felt that as the person almost shot, he should have the biggest say.

"Oh," Chris said nervously, looking like he wanted to hide from all the staring, "I'm fine."

Since he had narrowly avoided death-by-gunman just minutes before, and none of the crew knew that this was becoming a regular occurrence for Chris, nobody believed him. Maddison was too worried to let

Chris shrug this off. With her folded arms and scowl, Carrie felt similarly. Chris looked hopefully to them, realized he wasn't getting any help, and turned back to Bethy. "But it was much better than the last time I was menaced by an angry, gun-wielding person?" he tried.

This was clearly not as reassuring as he had hoped. Bethy made a small whimpering sound and sat back against a convenient tree trunk and one of the camera operators made a lunge in the direction of his tent, muttering about "open container laws be damned," and had to be grabbed by his friend. Redd, who was either more perceptive than previously suspected, or graced with a much darker sense of humor, genuinely smiled at them from his uncomfortable position next to the prone Harry. Carrie pinched the bridge of her nose and punched Chris very gently on the arm.

"Chris, remember how we had that talk about not throwing curveballs into the conversation?" Carrie asked.

"No?" Chris said.

"Aaargh."

"But Carrie and Maddison and I are all fine," Chris continued brightly while Carrie kicked a tree branch in irritation. "So we can all just go our separate ways and no harm done, right?"

The camera operator who'd been holding his friend back gave Chris a long, considering look, and released his death grip.

"Finally! Anyone else want something—ow!"

Karen the makeup artist and camera operator had amazing aim.

"We should get contact information from at least one of you," Redd said thoughtfully. "And I wouldn't mind if Flo took a quick look at Chris to make sure he isn't about to drop dead of delayed-onset heart attack or something, but if we don't press charges—"

"We aren't pressing charges?" Bethy asked.

"The main victim here is Harry," Redd said as if it was obvious. "And Chris, of course, but Chris doesn't seem that bothered, so as long as we pay for the damages without hitting up the insurance company and get the show done on time I don't see why we'd need to."

He looked up and around at the gathered crowd, and Maddison was unexpectedly relieved to find everyone nodding. Some of them a little reluctantly, true, but everyone was nodding.

"I . . . there are gaping holes in that plan," Bethy said, but she looked determined instead of defeated. There was a little color creeping back into her cheeks. "And I think Harry needs to take a decent vacation—a nice *long* vacation, and *how* are we going to get the entire shoot done with only two cameras, oh heavens . . . " Now she looked faintly overwhelmed, but that, Maddison was learning, was Bethy's default setting.

"Ooh," Chris said, "I know, you should—"

"*No!*" Carrie yelped.

"Do it all handheld!" Chris finished innocently.

Redd, at least, got the joke, if the way he doubled over laughing was anything to go by.

In the end, they went with the zipped-into-a-sleeping-bag option for Harry—he regained consciousness long enough for Redd to give him one of his sleeping pills, tell him everything was going to be fine, and jam the zipper of the sleeping bag after zipping it securely all the way up on Harry. Why Redd thought giving a previously unconscious person a sleeping pill was a good idea was then the subject of brief and furious debate before Flo reassured everyone that Harry had not had a concussion, that Harry would be fine, and that Redd was an idiot.

"We already knew that!" Bethy said, throwing up her arms, but then she'd gone off to worry over cameras and to file contact information.

They had actually given Bethy their contact information just that morning, since she had been the one to dig out a sheaf of waivers left over from the last attempt to let a contest-winning fan meet the cast and crew, and had found a working pen for Chris, Carrie, and Maddison to sign them with.

"What happened last time?" Carrie had asked, when Bethy didn't snatch the sticky note with "never again" scribbled on it off the folder fast enough.

"Terrible things," Bethy had said, "like dive-bombing owls. Just don't ask."

Because Carrie and Maddison had packed their things up before the little incident with Harry and the gun, they really could have accepted a granola bar and an apple and booked it in about five minutes. But Redd had been serious when he said he wanted Flo to give Chris a quick once-over, so Maddison and Carrie ended up sitting at the picnic table next to the television star, waiting for the caterer who was also the certified nurse to give them the okay.

They were joined only by Redd, since everyone else was arguing over the cameras and the best way to use the remaining cameras to film an entire show.

"Do you usually have everyone pulling double duty

like this?" Carrie asked Redd, and he laughed and shook his head.

"Yes, and this is one of the things that was driving Harry crazy," he explained. "We can't afford half the crew we really need, and we can't attract them anyway because nobody wants to work for us, so the people who *haven't* left keep having to take on more roles. It's because of the economy," Redd added solemnly, and Carrie snorted.

But then they fell into silence, Maddison nibbling on a granola bar and swinging her legs just for something to do, and Redd was now sneaking glances, carefully as possible, at Carrie. Maddison would maybe have chalked it up to the rampant paranoia that started with Chris and was catching, except Carrie was fidgeting under the attention. And Redd was trying extremely hard not to let on he was trying to sneak glances, and really this was getting ridiculous.

"Carrie," Maddison whispered, because whispering seemed appropriate. "Do you have something invisible on your face? It's distracting Redd."

Not her best line, true, but it did the trick. Carrie laughed and Redd jumped guiltily.

"Sorry," he said. "Forgive me my woolgathering. You look frighteningly like someone I used to know."

"Really," Carrie asked. "Who?"

"Oh," Redd laughed. "It's a long story and not a fun one. Not something you burden the youth of America with at any rate. You just . . . "

"I just what?" Carrie was doing her best to be gentle. Redd just looked at her. Really looked at her, like he was trying to memorize her face or compare it to some mental image, and it was edging back into awkward territory when Chris fought his way free of Flo and Redd shook his head and the spell broke.

"He's disgustingly healthy!" Flo yelled from inside the tent. "Now get out and let me make sandwiches in peace!"

"You just look like someone I used to know," Redd said lightly to Carrie, hopping to his feet. He flourished an arm. "And the setting, the summer sun, and the trees are all adding to the illusion. You three are a strange and charming sight, and I wish you all the best," he added. "Just be careful out there in the woods. You never know what's going to happen."

CHAPTER EIGHT

AFTER THE EXCITEMENT OF THE MORNING IT WAS almost a relief to get back on the trail, and return to forging down a partially overgrown hiking trail while listening to the peaceful buzzing of bugs in the woods. Chris was *almost* able to pretend that he wasn't shaky with adrenaline from his second near-brush with death, but Carrie knew him too well, and Maddison was scarily perceptive. Or just a very lucky guesser. She linked an arm in his in a disappointingly platonic manner and refused to let him slump to the floor of the state park and become one with the ferns and passing snakes, and instead insisted on talking about, of all things, ice cream. Ice-cream cones, to be exact.

"I'm just saying," Maddison said, helping Chris over a short trunk blocking the path, "there is no reason anyone should ever eat cake cones."

"But you can set them down on a flat surface," Chris protested. Carrie was humming a waltz behind them. "You can't do that with a waffle cone."

"You can't usually do it with a cake cone, either," Maddison pointed out. "They get soggy, or they tilt, or they have some little defect in the seam—and what kind of ice cream accessory has a *seam*? And then you're stuck holding a soggy, cardboard-flavored ice-cream holder, but it's technically edible so you feel guilty if you don't eat it."

"I'd never thought about it like that," Chris said. He actually *liked* the way cake ice-cream cones tasted.

"Oh, and that's another thing," added Maddison, now on a roll. "Who sets their ice cream down and leaves it for later?"

"What if someone wants to have melted ice-cream soup?" Chris offered.

"Then they should put it in a bowl, Chris."

Chris opened his mouth to point out the convenience of not having any dishes to wash when you had an ice-cream cone, but was interrupted by Carrie, who stopped, grabbed them both by the collars of their shirts, and declared that if she had to listen to two people argue about ice cream she was going to do so while eating some.

"And do either of you see any ice cream?" Carrie demanded. Chris decided that forging ahead of Carrie so she would go slower because of her foot was less fun than following behind her at a meandering pace. Hiking with Carrie was always going to be slightly unnerving.

"I think we're giving Carrie cravings," he told Maddison. "New topic?"

"Yep. So how do you feel about salads?"

"*Guys*," Carrie groaned.

"How about this," Maddison said, sobering. "Chris,

did you hear the conversation between Carrie and Redd while you were trying to convince a medical professional that you were perfectly fine just minutes after almost getting shot?"

"I did, actually," Chris said. "Did he give us a cryptic warning right there at the end or am I just imagining things again?"

"I'm not sure," Carrie said. They were picking their way through a soggy patch and for a moment they were too busy watching out for snakes to talk, but when they hit drier land Carrie picked the conversation back up. "I'd almost call it a *friendly* warning."

"You know, I think you're right," Chris said, and then jumped when Carrie flicked a twig at his shin. "What?"

"You suspect *everyone*, but we meet a terrible television host and you decide he's actually not that bad?"

"I—well, he isn't," Chris said, thinking partly of film cameras and mostly of how willing Redd had been to throw himself into the middle of a standoff to help.

"I'm going to agree with Chris," Maddison added.

"Redd was nice. Kind of flakey but really nice. And he's practically the first person who's acted like our suspiciousness is normal, and I'm definitely going to start watching his show regularly. What I want to know is what he saw in Carrie. Do you look frighteningly like a secret enchanted portrait?"

"No," Carrie said. "Although I've been told I look a lot like Aunt Elsie when she was young."

"Huh," Maddison said. And she looked like she was about to ask another question but a fat raindrop suddenly plopped on her head and she jumped and looked up. The morning had started bright, with fat, puffy clouds in a blue sky, but it must have been steadily clouding over because the sky was now a dull, hazy gray.

"Oh, that's not good," Carrie said, as another scattering of raindrops fell. "It wasn't supposed to do this!"

They had been winding around fewer and fewer trees and the groundcover had transitioned to beach grass while they had been arguing about ice-cream cones and Robin Redd. While squinting at the oncoming rain, Chris thought he saw in the distance . . .

"Is that the old Mission?" he asked, pointing.

It was.

"So, if we just head over casually," Carrie started to say, but then there was a threatening crack of thunder and caution was abandoned in favor of getting to the ruins before it started pouring.

They made it to the ruins in record time, despite the path being so windy, and were quickly standing in the dampening dust at the side of the equestrian path, reading the plaque identifying the mission.

"Ruins dating to the seventeenth century, believed to have been erected by some of the first Spanish settlers to the region," Maddison read aloud. "I notice they didn't identify it as a church."

"They probably didn't know," Carrie said. "I mean, does it look like a church?"

It didn't. It looked like a pile of very old stones and some weathered wood, clinging to the vague shape of a building by sheer stubbornness. It had once been large but a good quarter of the structure had collapsed, so that nothing but an outline of the foundation in crumbling foundation stones could be seen. There were hardly any windows left, and the doorway had flowers growing over it. Honestly, it was amazing that the church even still had a bit of its original wood-shingled roof, sagging towards the ground in the middle and dotted with holes.

"*Sooo*," Chris said, tapping his fingers on the plaque. "How do we get in there and find the parish register?"

"Walk in through the front door?" Carrie suggested, and then they all jumped at a tremendous crack of thunder as the heavens finally opened and it started to pour. "Quick, get inside!" Carrie gasped, and they were lucky the park service didn't fence off their delicate archeological sites, because if there had been a fence around the building Chris would have gone right through it.

As it was, he bypassed the flower-covered doorway and instead charged through the gaping hole in the side of the building and found himself in a cool, dark, cavernous space, dripping wet and trespassing on government property. *Creepy* government property—the inside of the old mission church was one big, dim, dusty cavern. The fact that it was completely open on one side didn't make it much lighter inside and the rain was dripping in through some of the holes in the roof. They'd darted into the most covered part of the old church and were clustered in what Chris, if he had to guess, would say was where the altar had once been. The floor here was wooden, more intact than anywhere else, and slightly raised. It was also covered in an ancient layer of splintered wood and stone dust from when the roof had tried to fall in and gotten only halfway down. But at least it was dry?

"Wow," Maddison said, following Chris and Carrie in and dumping her backpack in a mostly dry corner. "Listen to it out there. I hope it lets up before we need to head back."

"I hope we find the parish register," Carrie said, poking at a lump of lumber that was either a rotted wooden chair or a collapsed lectern. "Anybody have any ideas?"

"Find the cellar?" Maddison suggested.

That was easier said than done. The old mission church was half derelict and had been abandoned to the elements for years, and they spent a good twenty minutes—according to Chris's watch—poking around in the debris looking for a parish register or even just a bookshelf but coming up empty. There were some very old wooden benches sinking into the dirt floor and some optimistic weeds trying to grow wherever there was a big enough hole in the roof to let in sunlight, but not a piece of paper or book anywhere.

The walls, made of rough stone and with no crevices or hidden rooms, were barely standing; the rafters were exposed but held nothing but cobwebs and one very annoyed pigeon. The only chest in the room proved to have nothing in it but an old wasp nest. Chris was unpleasantly reminded of the last time they'd tried looking for the parish register, and tried to squash the sudden prickling at the back of his neck. He hadn't noticed any signs that they were being followed, but that *could* just mean someone was being careful.

Or it could mean that whoever was following them hadn't been fooled by their sneaking off at all, and instead had taken one look at the old mission church, decided that there couldn't be anything remotely worth looking for in it, and gone home where it was warm and dry. But no matter how hard Chris tried to tell himself that, the feeling that they were being followed—which Chris simply couldn't shake no matter how illogical it was or how much he pushed it to the back of his mind—suggested otherwise.

"Maybe there's an old well somewhere on the property," Maddison suggested, interrupting Chris's woolgathering and turning over one of the many fallen shingles with her shoe.

"Oh," Carrie sighed, wandering across the altar area towards the far wall and a window-like hole. "I *hope* we don't have to fall in another"—she froze.

"Carrie?" Chris asked.

"Something just creaked," Carrie hissed. She'd

frozen in mid-step and looked horrified. Chris, closest to her and reasonably sure that he was on solid ground, reached out and grabbed her arms, then pulled her over to him. They overbalanced and landed in a heap on a particularly lumpy piece of floor but nobody plummeted down a sudden hole to their deaths, so Chris decided to count it as a win.

"Was it a hollow creak?" Chris asked his cousin as she got to her feet and he rubbed his tailbone, which had only just started to lose the bruises from when he'd fallen into the cistern. Carrie nodded and Chris looked around for—*oh, that'll do nicely*, he thought. He grabbed a loose piece of wood and rapped the floor where Carrie had been standing, listening for an echo that was hollow. Which would mean that the floor itself was hollow. And if it was hollow, Chris thought, then that meant there was a hidden space underneath it, or at least a natural nook or cranny into which somebody might decide to stuff something secret. "Hmm," said Chris, and dropped to the floor to look for unusual seams.

"Chris is communing with the floor again," Maddison sighed, but she joined him and a second later Carrie followed them, knocking on the floorboards and listening for a difference in the thunking sounds. They almost gave up; the altar area was less decrepit than the rest of the mission church and the boards used to construct it were sturdy. Then one of the boards made a slightly hollower sound when hit, and they all started frantically sweeping years of dust and dirt away, and it was Carrie who actually found it, blowing years worth of dust out of an extra-large crack between the floorboards and inching her fingers into the crack until the resulting trapdoor came up with a painful groan.

"Whoa," Carrie said when she'd dragged the heavy door up and over, fishing a flashlight out of her pocket. The flashlight's beam illuminated a tiny room, barely big enough for the desk and the two rough shelves piled with papers that had been stuffed into it. It was dug directly into the earth itself, was just big enough for a person Chris's size to spin in a circle with their arms outstretched, and had dirt walls buttressed with wooden planks. "Jackpot!" Carrie hissed triumphantly. "Here, let me down?"

Of the three of them she was the smallest, so it made sense. It made even more sense, Maddison pointed out before Chris could figure out a way to lower Carrie down, to check if the hidden office space had a ladder.

"Hidden office space?" Carrie asked, circling the rim of the hole all the way around with her flashlight. Chris got up to grab his backpack from the pile they'd left in the corner—glancing nervously through the gap in the wall at the tree line he could barely see through a sheet of rain, wishing he didn't feel so much like someone was watching him—and tried to find his own flashlight, which was no longer in the spot he usually stored it. *Next time,* he thought to himself, stuffing spare socks back into the side pocket before they escaped, *volunteer to pack the bags so you don't have to ask Carrie where everything is.*

"Secret cave? Hidden archive? Private library?"

Maddison offered. She was leaning over the edge as far as possible and blowing ineffectively at the cobwebs lacing the shelves. "I don't know if there's a word for 'hidden compartment with a desk and bookshelves in it' in the dictionary—oh hey, you found it!"

"Yeah," Carrie agreed, flashlight wavering on a series of wooden boards nailed to the wall of the cavern. "But I almost think it would be better just to jump."

"Wait, do you have belt loops?" Chris asked, socks forgotten. "Or something to clip a carabiner to?" Maybe it was a good thing Carrie and Maddison had been the ones to pack up the contents of his pack so that it had gotten jumbled: Chris had completely forgotten that he had a carabiner and a length of climbing rope in his backpack. He held them up triumphantly. Maddison looked delighted. Carrie gave the belt loops on her jeans a cautious tug but she didn't say the plan was terrible.

"I'm just not sure we should clip anything to these pants," she explained. "They're kind of old and some of the belt loops have already started to fray." Carrie gave one a very firm tug and it made a ripping noise.

Maddison suggested just tying the rope around Carrie's waist; Carrie protested the waste if they couldn't get the knot out—which was nice of her, the rope and the carabiner had been expensive—and they finally settled on clipping the rope to Carrie's mostly emptied backpack and then buckling the backpack's front straps to make an improvised harness. With added storage space for the parish register, Maddison pointed out before Chris could convince himself that telling Carrie she looked like she was wearing a backpack leash was a good idea.

It turned out to be way more precaution than they needed, because Carrie made it all the way down the crude ladder without falling or slipping or having the ancient wood crumble under her touch, and there weren't even any booby traps.

"I don't think that is ever going to be an issue here," Maddison said, patting Chris on the back. He'd only realized they might run into booby traps *after* Carrie had started carefully pulling sheaves of paper off the shelves to look for parish registers.

"I can't believe that slipped my mind," Chris told Maddison. "What if there had been?"

"But there weren't, and I think we're dealing with a part of this mystery that nobody's tried to protect before." Maddison paused when Chris frowned at her, because if the parish register was down there then people had *killed* for the information it contained and that was basically the definition of something you booby-trapped. "I mean, I think we're the first people to find this, and I don't think the person who left this stuff here—an overworked parish priest moving stuff via ox cart or something, remember—thought it was important."

"So, we don't need to worry about booby traps on this end," Chris said. He was still watching Carrie nervously, although so far all she'd suffered was a sneezing fit.

"Not on this end, no," Maddison agreed. "Our

stalker has been quiet, though, so we should maybe check for booby traps on our way *out*."

"We should definitely check for booby traps on our way out," Carrie said, and Chris and Maddison stopped staring at each other and turned to Carrie, who had a heavy, leather-bound book clutched in her hands and a brilliant grin on her face.

"Did you find it?" Chris asked, almost falling into the hole trying to get a closer look.

"*Santa Maria, Estrella del Mar, registro de la parroquia,*" Carrie said. "I think this is it. The handwriting is tough to read and parts of it look like they're in Latin. But the date on the first couple of entries"— she opened the front cover and held it out—"matches what we need, so I'm thinking it's possible . . . " She shrugged. "Plus it's the only *book* down here, everything else looks like letters and maybe some maps."

"So, we grab this and we hide it," Chris said, opening his *Guide to Invasive Florida Wildlife* and peeling the Ziploc bag of acid-free paper from between the pages for the entry on anacondas. "What?" he added, because Maddison was grinning at him and Carrie was giving him an exasperated look. "I wanted to be prepared!"

"So you brought acid-free paper to wrap the book in?" Carrie asked, passing the book up to Chris and climbing out of the hole after it. "Where did you even find the paper?"

"I had some lying around in case of emergencies, where did you think I got it? And I feel bad enough running around in the rain with a fragile book that should be off in a box in an archive somewhere," Chris said, devoting himself to wrapping. The parish register was bigger than he'd thought and it took four sheets of paper just to get it securely wrapped. And it was still pouring outside, so he added his rain poncho on top of the paper, making a huge but hopefully protected bundle. "I didn't even think there'd be so many *other* papers down there."

"The sealed underground conditions probably helped preserve them," Carrie agreed, settling cross-legged at the edge of the hole. "Which, yeah, we just disturbed that environment, so we need to tell someone about this before the rest of the papers are ruined," she said. "Hey, do you think the archive takes anonymous tips?"

"Well, the *police* do," Maddison said dubiously. "And it might be a good idea to call them too. Or first. Or from a cell phone while we're walking back, except I was getting one bar off and on when it wasn't completely clouded over," she added, glancing out one of the half-fallen windows at the pouring rain still coming down in sheets and obscuring anyone who might be hiding.

"Okay, but first can somebody untie my backpack?" Carrie asked, and Maddison had to save them all from Chris's knots.

Then they took a moment to check phones, and Maddison was right: she didn't have any bars, Carrie had one, and Chris for some reason had two so he was elected to keep his phone on-hand in case of emergencies. Then a fat drop of rain made it through the roof and plopped cheerfully on the desk in the secret library and Chris decided to close the trap door before they got rain on decades-old papers.

"Quietly," Carrie hissed, as Maddison helped Chris tug the trapdoor back over. "What if they hear the trap door closing?"

"Then we just have to make it look like nobody's touched it," Maddison said. When it was closed, the trapdoor was practically invisible. The hinges disappeared and the whole thing sat exactly level with the rest of the wooden floor, matching right down to the wood grain. Maddison stood back to study it and then said, "Dust."

"Dust?"

"Or dirt," Maddison amended. "We should rub some dirt into the edges of the trapdoor," she explained, using a chip of wood to brush out the one spot where her hands had left trails in the floor's decades-old dust layer. "And then maybe walk across the edges randomly so nobody can tell where we disturbed it."

"Dust it is," Chris said, and wandered over to one

of the busted windows, where the shutters had fallen in and collected a pile of dry dust. He grabbed two handfuls from behind a large piece of shutter, figuring it would even hide the evidence that they were rearranging the dust in the old church, and brought them over to where Maddison was sprinkling pinches of dust over her handprints.

"Thanks," Maddison said, and sneezed.

"Guys," Carrie said, and her voice was so alarmed that Chris dropped his dust. "I just found footprints."

She'd wandered in the opposite direction Chris had, towards the end of the church that was without a roof at all, and was staring at a spot on the ground right where they'd entered. When Chris and Maddison joined her, Maddison discreetly blowing her nose, she pointed.

There were *two* sets of footprints, one about Chris's size and one slightly bigger, and both pointing into the church, clearly made by two people walking off the path and directly into the church after a somewhat heavy rain. But much more importantly, they were clearly pressed into dirt that was *no longer muddy*, and Chris ordered his pounding heart to calm down because it wasn't as bad as it looked.

"These are old," Chris said, poking the bigger one with his finger to be sure. Part of a ridge crumbled when he did. "Must have been made after a really heavy storm when the wind was blowing at an odd angle; this part of the building is pretty well shielded from rain." Which was true, their current downpour had slowed to a steadily decreasing patter and the wind had died down but it had been raging before and the spot where they were standing was still dry.

"But not *that* old," Carrie said. "These are obviously tennis shoes. In fact, I think they might be the same brand Chris likes to wear."

"Really?" Chris asked, and stood on one leg to look at his foot. Except he'd forgotten he was wearing his *hiking boots* so it turned into a pointless balance exercise because his boot prints didn't match either of the ones they'd found, and both Carrie and Maddison's feet were much too small. He hopped in a circle, put his foot down, and noticed that Carrie's mystery deepened: the footprints picked up again in the dust just inside the door, now illuminated by one brave little ray of sunshine. Then they went up to the remains of the altar, walked along the very outside edge of it, and came back down the other side of the church in what Chris had to admit was a nicely thought-out search pattern that also kept as close as possible to load-bearing walls. "Whoever this was," Chris said to Carrie when he'd finished following the footprints around and had determined that they didn't lead to someone hiding in the ruins, "they were smart."

"And they were looking for something," Carrie said. She was peering worriedly out at the trail while Maddison walked across the edges of the trapdoor.

"Probably?" Chris offered, shrugging. "They either had a better search pattern than we do or they were the most boring trespassers ever, why else would you sneak into an abandoned ruin in a state park and then do one nice safe loop around the perimeter?"

"You never know," Maddison said. "Boring people

sometimes like to have wild nights of rule-breaking too. Do me a favor and walk over the trap door once or twice? Carrie already did and I think she wants to head out."

"The sun's out," Carrie said apologetically. Chris hurried over to the trapdoor and wandered around it twice, then hoped it was sturdy enough and walked right across it once. He didn't fall in, so it must have been sturdy. "And it's practically noon, if we want to get back to the trailhead at one like we promised Dr. McRae we need to start soon. And that thing will creak when I step on it but it doesn't mind you stomping over it?"

"I don't stomp," Chris said as primly as he could.

CHAPTER NINE

CARRIE WAITED UNTIL THEY WERE MARCHING DOWN the trail, sending butterflies scurrying away from puddles, before she brought the topic back to the footprints they'd found in the abandoned church. Of course, she brought up the topic by saying, "So, who do you think was in the church before us, and when?" which made Chris miss a step—he had been thinking longingly of a hot meal and a shower—and narrowly avoid stomping a butterfly.

"Aaaggh . . . stalker number one?" Chris said.

"Number one?" Carrie asked.

"Yeah!" Chris said. "I hate naming things and then

finding out that there was actually more than one, so for now whatever mysterious person is lurking behind the scenes watching us is stalker number one."

Maddison cast a reflexive glance into the trees.

Chris continued, "But if we find out that it's a team—"

"Based on the fact that there were two sets of footprints," Carrie interrupted. "*If* we assume that the footprints are even connected to the person stalking us, which we can't yet."

"Because obviously someone else was running around in the park at some unspecified moment in time and just *happened* to explore the same building we needed to really carefully," Maddison said with a bit of sarcasm.

"Then the next person is stalker number two, and so on and so forth," Chris continued. "And if not, then stalker number one sounds cool anyway, so they can't go after me for giving them a silly name."

"I think they're going to go after you for something

other than the name you give them," Carrie said. "Like, oh, the lost treasure of the *San Telmo*."

"Okay, true," Chris sighed. "But I feel like we have more questions than answers again. We found the parish register, even though we can't read it."

"Not *yet*," Carrie said. "I have a Spanish dictionary and a Latin dictionary, and I already asked Father Michaels to help me translate. We'll figure it out!"

"But we still don't know who might be following us, we discovered that two people searched the church before we did, we got tangled up in a film crew, and we didn't even see a ghost!"

"Did you . . . want to see a ghost?" Maddison asked.

"I don't know!" Chris said. "I was just really disappointed that the bloody handprints turned out to be corn syrup handprints laid out by a film crew!"

"Aw, cousin," Carrie said, giving him a very uncomfortable side-hug. "It's okay, we still got to the register before anyone else. That has to count for *something*."

"And, um, I wasn't going to say anything," Maddison said, "but you do know that the camera crew only confessed to planting *one* handprint, right? They left the one at the picnic area, because Todd knew they were going to film there later today. Nobody said anything at all about the one we saw from the side of the trail."

"They didn't?" Suddenly Chris was very aware that they had been wandering around in a supposedly haunted woods for two days, and remembered, unbidden, that Annie Six-Fingers had very little patience.

"No," Maddison said. "And I didn't think to ask about it. I told Bethy about the one at the picnic area, and she yelled at Todd until he confessed to the one at the picnic area. Nobody said anything about the one off the side of the trail, *which wasn't somewhere they were filming.*"

"Oh, hey!" Carrie exclaimed. The staring into the woods looking for ghosts was starting to get ridiculous, and she had taken a peek at her phone. "I have *two* bars now!"

The tension shattered and they started walking

again, Chris and Maddison pulling out their own phones and Carrie pulling up her contacts list.

"I've got one whole bar," Maddison said, just as Carrie tapped a button and held her own phone to her ear. "Who are you calling?"

"Professor Griffin," Carrie said.

"Huh." Maddison shrugged and called someone herself.

"Oh, nice," Chris said. "Ignore me in favor of the phone." But it was actually a good idea: when you were hiking, the trip back always seemed shorter than the trip there, and today was no exception. They were only about twenty minutes from the trailhead and had made it this far without being attacked for the book or by an angry ghost, so it would be a shame to ruin the streak of good luck by getting kidnapped mere minutes from home.

It was also the last point where stalker number one might try something out of sight of prying eyes. Carrie and Maddison both being on the phone with an adult was an insurance measure to ward off possible attacks, although . . . Chris stepped up his pace so that he was walking next to Maddison and in front of Carrie. As the only person not on the phone he would be the best option for grabbing.

And I would call someone, Chris thought to himself, *but Carrie and Maddison have taken the only two adults who know our secret and there is nobody left for me to call.*

In a perfect world, of course, he would be calling Aunt Elsie, who couldn't go camping as often as she liked because of work but would be delighted to hear about the ghost, and the film crew, and the parish register. And who would absolutely have believed them about the secret and the treasure. But Aunt Elsie was gone, and could only look down on them from somewhere up high and full of correctly archived masterpieces, and Chris was left listening to half of two conversations at once and trying not to see ghosts in the woods where there weren't any.

"No, really, it went well," Maddison was saying to her dad. "I don't swoon at movie stars and anyway

147

Robin Redd isn't my type. No, I—yes, there is more to the story than that, I just don't want to tell you over the phone so I'm saving it for when we get home and I can have . . . no you *didn't*. *Dad*! That was *my* cereal, you don't even *like* that brand!"

So apparently Dr. McRae had a thing for breakfast cereals. Meanwhile, Carrie's conversation had consisted mostly of the words "yes" and the phrase "everyone is fine" with more or less emphasis as the situation warranted, meaning that Professor Griffin had been worried.

"Yes, we are fine," Carrie was saying again. "Yes, everyone is fine, no, nobody died, nobody got eaten by a shark, nobody—how were you expecting us to overdose on alcohol in the woods?"

Ah. Professor Griffin must be reading aloud from the list of "things Professor Griffin was not allowed to let Kingsolvers do on pain of having his captain's hat fed to the alligators." Officially it was the list of "things that good friends do not let Kingsolvers do on pain of being fed to the alligators." It was a very long list that had been started by Chris's great-grandmother after one too many broken Kingsolver bones, and had some strangely specific prohibitions on it, including the rule that you should never try to send Kingsolvers to the moon. As far as Chris knew there had never been an astronaut in the family. As for Professor Griffin, he was more frightened by the idea of watching alligators eat his hat then the idea of being eaten himself.

Carrie was still reassuring Professor Griffin that they had not done any of the things on the list, and lying through her teeth because both "trespass on government property" and "appear on a reality television show" were on that list, when they rounded the very last bend and hit the parking lot. Maddison had actually hung up five minutes previously, after telling her father, "We're about five minutes out, I'll see you in a bit," in a voice that carried. Then she'd joined Chris in listening to Carrie's conversation in amusement.

"Oh, hi!" Carrie said into the phone, and waved. Across the gravel parking lot, Professor Griffin waved back. He was sitting on the picnic bench with a box of muffins, his captain's hat pulled low over his eyes, grinning at them.

"Smaller Kingsolvers!" he declared, hopping to his feet and striding towards them. "You're unharmed! I was reasonably sure, but you never can tell until you count all the limbs." Carrie laughed and gave Professor Griffin a hug, which he returned delightedly. Then he poked her backpack. "Find anything interesting? You were so happy on the phone that I assumed—you're much less chipper when your missions fail to turn up the goods—but again, you never can count the chickens until you've bought the coop."

Chris tried very hard to find a deeper meaning in that comment before he gave up. Professor Griffin sometimes had gloriously creative sayings and sometimes mixed regular sayings up so horribly that their meaning was impossible to find even with a magnifying glass, and he did both with equal frequency. Instead, Chris patted his own backpack, which was currently mostly full of parish register.

"Brilliant!" Professor Griffin said. He put an arm

around both Chris and Carrie and steered them towards the waiting cars. "Do you know," the professor continued, "that I just had a talk with Abigail and *Moby* needs another outing?"

Abigail was Professor Griffin's most responsible grad student and the person who actually kept track of *Moby*. As *Moby* was a small submersible, it didn't actually need outings like a dog needed walks to the park, so what Abigail had actually meant was that Professor Griffin needed to get his permanently malfunctioning submersible to collect useful data before it was set loose in the college swimming pool again.

"If you've already made plans, it's no bother," Professor Griffin continued, spinning his captain's hat with one hand, his other hand on his hip. "But if you need a boat for the next leg of your adventures I'm willing to volunteer my own humble vessel."

Chris was so relieved at the next hurdle to their investigation evaporating on its own that he could do nothing but gape at Professor Griffin, and Carrie had to elbow him.

"I—oh wow, yes, that would be *great, thank you!*" Chris stammered. Carrie beamed at Professor Griffin.

"I told you it wouldn't be an issue," Maddison said. She'd hung back a little shyly when Professor Griffin hijacked the conversation, and at the sound of her voice Professor Griffin gave an exaggerated jump and stared at her. "A smallish not-Kingsolver," he said, squinting at Maddison like she was a new and unusual species. "Whoever might you be?"

"Maddison," Maddison said politely, shaking hands and looking at Professor Griffin curiously. She didn't even get too weirded out when he switched from shaking her hand to giving it a very old-fashioned kiss, which he did sometimes. It tended to go over better with smaller kids than with Chris and Carrie's teenage friends, and Maddison was winning major bonus points. Most of Chris and Carrie's friends thought Professor Griffin was too weird to talk to.

"I'm new," Maddison said when she finally got her hand back. "It's nice to meet you. I've heard a lot about you."

"Well, clearly a new, good thing, right Chris?" Professor Griffin asked, grinning even more widely at the way Chris and Maddison both blushed. "And you've only heard the good things about me?" he asked. Maddison nodded, smiling. "It's lovely to meet you, Maddison," Professor Griffin said. "I was just talking to your father. We work in some of the same places but we almost never get to chat!"

Dr. McRae, the smaller presence in any area with Professor Griffin in it, gave them a half smile and a wave in greeting. He was leaning against the side of his car, arms crossed over his chest, his expression weirdly blank. Suddenly, Chris remembered Maddison describing her father as having a purposefully blank expression, and understood what she meant. It was just as creepy in person as it had been in his imagination, and it was *not* in Chris's imagination that Dr. McRae looked worried as well as weirdly blank.

Dr. McRae moved from his post against the car with a heavy sigh. "We might not be working in the same place for a while," he said, finally wandering over toward them. He still had his arms crossed and his expression was now simply serious, and when he reached their excited and triumphant little clump he put a hand on Maddison's shoulder. "I got a call from a colleague in Montana last night."

"Montana?" Maddison asked. She'd been flushed with triumph and relief and very happy, but something about Montana made her suddenly puzzled and serious. "What's going on in Montana?"

"Nothing good, I'm afraid," Dr. McRae said. "It's—do you remember George?"

"George, from when I was a kid?" Maddison asked. "Yes, I remember George, what happened?"

"He's been in an accident and can't teach the rest of his summer classes," Dr. McRae said. "He's teaching two and he asked me to fill in for the rest of the week, or at least until he can find a long-term substitute, and the rest of the family—they could really use some support right now. And I can't say no to George. I owe him too much."

Maddison pressed both hands over her mouth, and

then closed her eyes. Dr. McRae turned to Professor Griffin with a brave smile, and one that Chris had absolutely no right to think was faked. "So I'm afraid I already talked it over with the board," Dr. McRae said. "They're putting Henderson in charge for the week and letting me take my week's vacation starting now. I feel horrible doing this to you so soon after I started this job, but George . . ."

"Well, that's terrible!" Professor Griffin said. "Of course you should go, take all the time you need, nobody at the Archive is going to complain about a situation like this. Will you have to leave your family?"

"That's the other thing," Dr. McRae said. Maddison sighed. She was dry eyed and fiddling with her braid. "I hate to do this to you, Maddison," Dr. McRae said, "but . . . you and mom are coming with me. I'm so sorry, I know it's a mess, I know you had other plans, but George asked for you and he might not have much time left."

"Oh dear," Professor Griffin said faintly. Carrie hissed in sympathy. Even Dr. McRae looked stricken, as though this was the last thing he wanted to have to tell his daughter.

"It's okay, Dad," Maddison said. She wasn't looking at anyone and was fiddling with the ribbon she'd pulled out of her hair. "I understand. It's going to *suck*, but . . . " She looked at Chris, really *looked* at him like she was willing him to read her mind. "I can't skip this," she said. "I'm really, really sorry, but I can't skip this. You're going to have to go without me."

There was something going on under the surface here, but Chris couldn't for the life of him figure out what it was. Except he was *certain* the McRaes did not really have to go to Montana to help a friend of Maddison's father. But Maddison looked determined, stricken, even, and Chris sensed that making a fuss was the worst possible thing to do. So he swallowed, and tried to smile, and told Maddison that of course it was fine, and that they would just be sorry not to have her around, and jumped a mile when Maddison suddenly tackled him in a hug before running to her car.

Dr. McRae looked at them all for a moment longer,

frowning. Then he made a move that was either an aborted attempt to shake Chris's hand or clap him on the back, and tucked his hands into his pockets. Then he smiled at Carrie, didn't even look at Professor Griffin, and said, "We *will* be seeing you," before he joined his daughter in the car and they pulled out of the parking lot in a shower of gravel.

Chris, Carrie, and Professor Griffin stood there, lost. Finally, Professor Griffin broke the spell by wandering back over to the picnic table and closing the lid on his box of muffins.

"Well, that was odd," he said. "I guess I should . . . take you two home?"

CHAPTER TEN

ODDER STILL WAS WHAT CHRIS FOUND IN HIS pocket when he was unpacking later that evening. He'd already hidden the parish register safely under his floorboards, in a proper acid-free box to protect it, and had managed to dodge most of his mother's well-meaning questions about the hike and if Maddison had liked the state parks and would she like to come over for dinner sometime this week? Declaring that he needed to go get his laundry sorted before the wet clothes in his bag started to mold was his excuse to escape. It was also how he discovered the clue Maddison had left him in one of his sweatshirt pockets.

He'd been wearing his sweatshirt tied around his waist for most of the hike back, because it had been slightly damp and he couldn't fit it in his backpack along with the parish register, and so it had been right there with convenient pockets when Maddison had hugged him. Which must have been when she had tucked her purple ribbon into the same pouch as his Tic Tacs, which he went to retrieve before washing the still-damp sweatshirt. He recognized it instantly: it was the same knotted purple ribbon last seen in a bow on the end of Maddison's braid.

"Maddison," Chris said to himself, stretching the ribbon out full length on his bedspread and staring at the knots she'd tied in it. "What are you trying to tell me?"

There were eleven knots in the ribbon, some small, some big, and in no particular order. Actually, Chris amended, some of the knots were longer than others. It had been a while since he'd done friendship bracelets but it looked like she'd done single and double half-hitch knots. They went – • – • – – • – – • • and they looked almost like SOS in Morse code except Chris knew what SOS in Morse code was and it was • • • – – – • • •, so what on earth was Maddison doing? Or had she just been tying knots in her hair ribbon out of nerves and Chris was misinterpreting the result?

He dragged an old book on knots out from under his dresser and looked up both single and double half-hitch knots, but there was nothing particularly meaningful about either, and Chris was at a loss. Nothing came to him while he threw all his wet things into the washing machine, or while he had a late dinner with his parents and tried not to talk about the hiking trip, or even when he sat down at his computer afterward and, still at a loss, tried investigating the footprints they'd found instead.

Chris had taken a picture of both of the mysterious footprints before they'd left the mission church, but unlike the crime scene investigators on the shows Carrie's mom pretended not to like he didn't learn anything. Aside from pulling out his own sneakers and confirming that the tread was similar but not exactly the same—which proved almost nothing because he had two pairs of sneakers that were different brands and the treads were both similar but not exactly the same—Chris didn't come to any interesting conclusions. If he had a police force's resources he might have gotten much further, but he didn't, and it turned out to be fruitless to Google "shoe treads." The top result—the top *five* results—showed pictures of novelty flip-flops that left words behind wherever you walked.

It did occur to him that the last time he'd been reading about codes in relation to string or ribbons it had been when he read up on the possible Incan practice of keeping records in the form of knots, but refreshing his memory on that subject just reminded him that nobody had yet figured out how to read those knots, which meant it was a *little* unlikely that Maddison would leave him a message in that format. But she was trying to tell him something! He was just looking up the alphabet in Morse code, on the off chance that she had spelled out an actual message on the ribbon—although it would have to be a message that was, at most, only four letters long—when Carrie turned up and scared him half to death again.

"It's CQD," she said from the window, and Chris yelped and fell off the side of the bed.

"Carrie! What are you doing? It isn't even *dark* yet!" It wasn't, it was only five thirty.

"Lurking," Carrie said unapologetically. She pushed the window open and wedged herself through. "I got done unpacking and wanted to check on you," she added. "That thing with Maddison and her dad was *weird*. And it must be even weirder than I thought," she added, "because that's CQD tied into Maddison's hair ribbon." Chris looked at the Morse code alphabet he'd looked up online, and then at the ribbon. It *did* spell out C, Q, and D.

"Okay, I'll bite," Chris said, handing over the ribbon when Carrie held out her hand for it. "What does CQD stand for?"

"Nothing," Carrie said. "But it was one of the very

first distress signals after they invented the radio," she added before Chris got a chance to protest. "People say it means stuff like 'Come Quick, Danger' or 'Come Quick, Drowning' or 'Seek You, Danger' but it really just means 'all stations, distress' so it's not that different from SOS. What?" she added when Chris stared at her. "I did a report on the *Titanic* once and it was mentioned in one of the books I read!"

That did not actually clarify anything, so Carrie sighed and elaborated. "It was one of the distress signals sent out by the wireless operator on the *Titanic*," she explained. "That's all."

"Okay," Chris said. "That makes sense—no, actually it doesn't, how do you get 'seek you, danger' out of the letters C, Q, and D?"

"It's phonetic!" Carrie said.

"And why did Maddison tie it into her hair ribbon and then sneak the ribbon into my pocket?" Chris asked.

"Right. Why didn't she use SOS?" Carrie added,

picking at one of the "long-dash" knots. "This is a much harder code to tie into a ribbon on the fly."

"Why did Dr. McRae snatch Maddison away like he thought we were about to get attacked and he didn't want his precious daughter anywhere near the blast radius?" Chris groaned, defeated.

"Oh good, I wasn't the only one who thought that," Carrie said, settling in Chris's desk chair. "You know, I have a theory, but you aren't going to like it."

"Tell me anyway?"

"SOS is almost universally a sort of . . . I don't know . . . 'Help, *I'm* in distress' sort of code," Carrie said, twirling the ribbon absently around her fingers. "Whereas CQD is older and doesn't have the same meanings to most people. One of the meanings people give the letters is 'seek you, danger' and that almost sounds more like a warning than a cry for help. So if you wanted to tell someone that *they* were in danger . . . "

"You think Maddison was warning us," Chris said. It wasn't a comforting thought.

"I think we'd better find the *San Telmo,* and fast," Carrie said, tugging at a knot of the ribbon. "Otherwise, terrible things are going to happen."

CHAPTER
ELEVEN

WHEN MADDISON HAD BEEN FIVE AND SIX AND seven and honestly all the way up to age twelve, she'd had a very vivid fantasy life involving a stuffed dinosaur named George. He had lived in Montana, when he wasn't visiting the McRaes for extended periods of time, and he was— young Maddison had told her father repeatedly and very seriously—a college professor, just like Daddy. George had had seven eggs back home, named Bob, Grill, Pumpkin, Splendid, Barbie, Dasher, and Seven, and he worked long hours at paper grading and tea partying to provide for them. Dasher had always been unable to fly, but a small and embarrassingly opinionated Maddison had insisted that if George saved up enough money he could have an operation to fix his wings. Maddison's father had taken George to work on three separate occasions so George could fill in for another teacher and earn a little extra salary, because Kevin McRae was a very patient parent and Maddison had been a small child with funny ideas about teaching.

The only terrible accident Maddison could think of involving a George would have to be related to Dasher, and this required a serious explanation. So she waited until her father's nervousness had gone down by half, which took him almost the entire drive home from the state park, and then gave him a little extra time to get relaxed before she pounced. It didn't help that he seemed to think they were being followed—her dad kept checking the rearview mirror and every time he did Maddison had to check, too—and Maddison had just spent two days in the woods afraid that *she* was being followed. But by the time they pulled onto their street her dad had relaxed and Maddison had calmed down some, so she took a deep breath and attacked the issue head on.

"Dasher's health took a turn for the worse, huh?" Maddison asked her dad as they were pulling into their driveway, and he sagged in his seat, caught somewhere between a laugh and a sob. As her dad was not the person who had just been the subject of the most awkward and suspicious "you may never see each other again" parting this side of *Romeo and Juliet* Maddison thought it rather unfair that he was the one getting hysterical, and she told him so, sternly.

"But you played your part to perfection, Mads," Maddison's father said. "I know you suspect me of being a spy, and I know you won't believe me when I tell you that I was never a spy, but I do hope you believe me when I tell you that *you* would be an excellent spy. You roll with things so well, and you can fake your way through just about anything."

"I have no poker face," Maddison pointed out, because it was true and because she had lost track of the conversation somewhere around the point her father had complimented her acting instead of defending his choices. Or explaining his choices, which were getting as complex and creative and paranoid as some of Chris's nuttier plots.

"Yes, but you're smart enough to make up for it," Maddison's father said. "I saw you put your hands over your mouth to cover—what were you hiding?"

"My hysterical urge to giggle," Maddison said grimly. "I wasn't expecting to be told that my favorite stuffed dinosaur was tragically dying and that we needed to go help take care of his kids—seriously, Dad, *what the heck is going on?*"

"I had to warn you without warning you," her dad said. "And I was afraid it wouldn't work. It's been years since you've talked about George, and people forget that sort of thing sometimes. You did magnificently, though, Mads."

"I still sleep with George on my pillow," Maddison said, as though that was the major problem with her life right now, even though it really wasn't. "Dad, *why are my dinosaurs having a family emergency?*"

"Because *we're* having a family emergency," her dad sighed, fiddling with his seatbelt. He finally opened the car door to get out. "I was lying about Montana, though, we're going to visit Gregory Lyndon for a week and he's in Nebraska."

"Why?" Maddison asked, following him out of the car.

"Because . . . I can't run from my past anymore," her dad said. "Not without it hurting you. So, this time I'm going to face it once and for all."

Which was . . . cryptic. As usual. Irritated, Maddison followed her dad up the short walk to their front door, where he paused and turned back.

"I was planning to visit Gregory Lyndon this week anyway," he said, hand on the doorknob, which he was studying intently. "But I wasn't planning to make you and Mom come with me. But then I had a conversation with Griffin this morning." He said "Griffin" with a slight hesitation. "Willis Griffin and I went to school together," Maddison's dad continued, as though he wasn't breaking open a deep, dark secret on the front porch in the middle of the afternoon. "And we—there was an incident we were both involved in and I still don't know how much he knew about it. He could have had nothing to do with it, he could have had *everything* to do with it, I just don't know. And until I do you aren't going anywhere with him. Unless I'm there," Maddison's dad amended. "I don't think he likes me very much anymore. He's always giving me dirty looks."

"Oh," Maddison said. And then, horrified, she added, "But then are Chris and Carrie in some kind of danger?"

"I don't think they're in any kind of danger," her dad told her. "I can't imagine Griffin harming them, he *adored* their aunt and he spends half his time telling people about their achievements like a proud uncle. But he had some sort of falling out with me after Ryan—" He stopped. "We had a falling out and it nearly ruined my life," he said instead. "I just can't trust him enough to leave you alone with him. But I'm not going to tell him that to his face, so I came up

171

with the family emergency on the spot. Your mother is probably furious, though. When I called her and asked about a plane ticket for you, she insisted on coming along, but you know how she hates packing."

Maddison's mother was actually grumbling at the refrigerator when Maddison and her father snuck inside, a growing pile of food that wouldn't last the week in the fridge on the counter next to her and her suitcase on the dining-room table. When she heard the door open she stood up, Tupperware container of mashed potatoes in one hand, and said, "Kevin, did you explain everything to Maddison?"

"On the front porch in broad daylight?" Maddison's dad said. "Um, no." Her mom sighed.

"You have until we leave Gregory's," she said, putting the potatoes in the "offer to the neighbors" pile. "Otherwise *I'm* telling Maddison everything, and since

I don't know how the love story part of your secret past went—"

"It was not a—okay! I'll explain it! Just not right now when we really need to go pack because our flight leaves at seven!" Maddison's dad was sneaking down the hallway towards her parents' bedroom as he spoke, and her mom made irritated shooing motions at him until he went in to pack.

"He does want to tell you," Maddison's mom told her, tugging the vegetable drawer open and wincing. "He really does, but everything that's happened in the past couple of weeks has scared him, and I think he's a little ashamed of what happened. So if your father can't get himself together and tell you why he almost didn't graduate from college on time by the end of this week, come find me and *I'll* do it, or if you want to ask Gregory, he has an unbiased outsider's report and was actually there. Now go pack, we have a plane to catch and I have to get someone to take our milk— he had to pull this on me right after I went grocery shopping . . ."

And then the McRae household turned into a war zone, because that was what always happened when they were trying to pack for a trip. It would help a lot if Maddison's father wasn't the sort of person who got things nicely folded and then left them out instead of putting them in his suitcase. They spent most of the evening chasing down lost pieces of Maddison's father's luggage and trying to figure out where his glasses were, with Maddison's father sitting on the couch guarding the suitcases while his wife and daughter tracked down everything that he couldn't find.

Which was how Maddison found herself in her parents' study, shifting papers on her dad's desk and wondering where she would hide if she were a pair of lost but necessary reading glasses.

"Paperweight, paperweight, paperweight, paperweight," Maddison muttered under her breath, "why does he have so many paperweights?" Plus, her dad tended to put paperweights down on papers and then put more papers down and put more paperweights on top of them until he had a many-layered booby trap just waiting for someone to move the wrong paper and bring everything down on their toes. It was like playing a complicated version of the game *Jenga*. Maddison considered the desk and then picked up two notebooks and a glass full of pens. Nothing happened. She let out the breath she'd been holding and moved a large blue glass paperweight. An overstuffed file folder tumbled off the desk, papers fanning out across the floor.

"Aargh," Maddison said, and plopped down on the floor to sweep them back up. The folder was old and battered, and the label had the letters THC written in the corner in faded pencil. Most of the papers were handwritten sheets of regular notebook paper that could be shuffled back into a pile, but when Maddison picked the pile up so she could square the edges, a shower of photos and small slips of cardboard fell out.

"Oh for Pete's sake," Maddison said, and went chasing after pictures and movie-ticket stubs. For square pieces of paper they sure scattered *everywhere*. Most of the pictures, when she gathered them up, turned out to be random candid snapshots of people Maddison didn't recognize, and there were a bunch of pictures of trees and bushes and buildings mixed in, with no clear rhyme or reason. No names on the back either, Maddison discovered when she peeked, although most of the pictures had numbers in one corner, as if they were part of a series or—Maddison froze in the act of shuffling through pictures. *Most* of the pictures were of people she didn't recognize, but she'd just found one that *was*.

A slight, heavily freckled redhead was yanking a weed out of somebody's garden in the picture, her hair falling over her shoulder in a braid and tangling with the bronze necklace she was wearing. She wasn't facing the camera, probably because she hadn't seen the camera or the person taking the picture, but it was hard to mistake Carrie even from the side.

Maddison shoved the picture into the middle of the stack and put the stack back into the folder, shaken. She trusted her dad, always had, but there were things you didn't do secretly, and taking pictures of your daughter's best friend without either of them knowing it was pretty high on that list of things that you didn't do. And she wanted to know the secret that kept her dad up at night and haunted him, whatever it was that made him so afraid that something terrible was going to happen to Maddison so that he'd taught her safety precautions more suited to the daughter of a president than the daughter of a college professor. But now . . .

Well, now Maddison was starting to wonder if knowing what her dad was afraid of would be worse than the ongoing agony of *not* knowing. And wondering just how deep and how far back the secret went. She'd given Chris her hair ribbon knotted into the Morse code for CQD because she was scared and he'd looked so lost, and because Maddison didn't want him to think that *she* wanted to leave Chris and Carrie to their own devices for the rest of the search for the *San Telmo*. She hadn't used SOS because—well, SOS was the obvious choice, and Maddison was just paranoid enough to worry that if the ribbon fell into the wrong hands someone would be able to figure it out. She was trusting Chris to figure out that the ribbon said

CQD and then know what CQD meant because he had once sent her a cypher in a series of text messages, so if anyone could figure it out it would be him.

But now Maddison was starting to wonder if her warning was more pointed than she'd thought. Could she be in danger? How much danger were Chris and Carrie in? How much worse was it going to get—and how much danger would Maddison put them all in if she tried to figure it out?

"You started this, you finish it," Maddison told herself, resolving to come to her own conclusions before she dragged Chris and Carrie into discussion, and then she put the folder back on the desk under its paperweight and finally found her dad's glasses, resting on the bookshelf next to the desk. "Just so long as it doesn't finish me," Maddison added, and flicked the lights off.

Back in the state park, at a beat-up aluminum picnic

table currently covered in camera pieces and coffee cups, Robin Redd was fixing his hat. He'd been wearing it when a sudden rainstorm blew up, and he and his hat had been drenched, which had made the feathers tucked into his hatband droop sadly. Redd had borne the shame of his hat bravely while they got all the filming they needed for the day, and hadn't even yelped when a snake slithered over his shoe, but as soon as they were done he had hurried off to fetch his sewing kit and the little collection of feathers he kept for just this sort of emergency.

Twilight was swiftly falling but there was still just enough light remaining for him to sit outside and attach the new feathers to his hat with a few neat stiches. He was humming away to himself and admiring the effect of a dyed purple feather next to a natural brown one when Bethy Bradlaw came up behind him and thwacked her notebook on the table. Redd's sewing supplies rattled and Redd himself jumped almost a foot in the air and pricked himself with his needle. He was jumpy today, but his producer had gone berserk earlier, so he had a right to be jumpy.

"Bethy!" Redd said, wondering why she looked irritated this time. Irritated and confused, and Bethy was often irritated and confused by the people she had chosen to spend her life working with but she didn't usually throw her notebook at them. Okay, there had been that one time, but David was a pest.

"Robin," Bethy asked patiently, "why did you take a Sharpie and mark out all my notes on the *San Telmo* segment?"

"Oh, that," Redd said guiltily. "It was a moment of weakness on my part when you were sending Harry off to your mom's. I was overreacting, it's *fiiine*."

"Sure it is," Bethy said, sitting down across from Redd. "Robin, what's wrong with the *San Telmo*?"

"Did you know the ship isn't even said to be haunted?" Redd asked, fiddling with the feathers on his hat. "A long-lost treasure ship, and not one single legend or scary story has formed around its figurehead or its crew or the mythical place where it landed! It's absurd!"

"So, you don't want to do a segment on the *San Telmo* because it *isn't* supposed to be haunted?" Bethy opened her binder and pulled out the worst sheet. It was nothing but a page of black lines. "This is going a little far, even for you."

Redd didn't want the explanation to come out but his mouth had other ideas, because he said, "Nobody looks for the *San Telmo* and comes away unharmed," before he could stop himself, and then since it was already out he gave in and told Bethy the rest.

"I had a friend in college who died looking for the *San Telmo*," Redd explained. "He just disappeared one day and was never seen again. It shattered those of us who knew him. There aren't any stories about the *San Telmo* being haunted," Redd said, "but the ship has to be cursed. It ruins the people who go looking for it. That's why I won't try anymore."

"Okay," Bethy said. "Thank you for telling me, but this is the sort of thing you let me know about when

I *start* researching the place we're shooting." Redd looked sadly down at his hat and she relented. "But I won't make you tempt fate by doing a piece on the *San Telmo*. Now come help me convince the network to send us looking for dolphins next month," she said, and swatted one of the growing number of mosquitos.

Redd lingered, gathering his hat and feathers, and when he was certain he was alone, he looked up at the sky, and at the moon just peeking through the clouds, and asked of someone who wasn't there: "My dear, what are you *doing?*"